"What part of 'The mob's got a contract on you' do you not understand?"

Dan's question didn't faze the stunning blonde. She shrugged. "I understand you're trying to do your job, Mr. FBI Special Agent Maddox, but you should remember I've lived with these people all my life."

He tried to press the point, but she cut him off.

"Do you really think they don't know where to find me? They have more arms into more places, people and things than a family of octopuses."

"How about this, Carlotta—"

"Hold it right there! I've asked you a million times not to call me that. Carlie. *Car-lie*. It's not that hard, is it? Try it—you might like it."

Her flirty wink nearly sent him over the edge. "Do you ever take anything seriously?"

"Yes," she said, her voice warm and vibrant. "I take God seriously. And then I leave the rest to Him."

"You go ahead and do that, but while you're in the witness protection program, you better leave the driving to me."

Books by Ginny Aiken

Love Inspired Suspense

Mistaken for the Mob #26
Mixed Up with the Mob #30
Married to the Mob #34

GINNY AIKEN,

a former newspaper reporter, lives in Pennsylvania with her engineer husband and their three younger sons—the oldest married and flew the coop. Born in Havana, Cuba, raised in Valencia and Caracas, Venezuela, she discovered books early, and wrote her first novel at age fifteen while she trained with the Ballets de Caracas, later known as the Venezuelan National Ballet. She burned that tome when she turned a "mature" sixteen. Stints as reporter, paralegal, choreographer, language teacher and retail salesperson followed. Her life as wife, mother of four boys and herder of their numerous and assorted friends, brought her back to books and writing in search of her sanity. She's now the author of twenty-one published works, a frequent speaker at Christian women's and writers' workshops, but has yet to catch up with that elusive sanity.

married to the mob

GINNY AIKEN

Steeple
Hill®

Published by Steeple Hill Books™

STEEPLE HILL BOOKS

Steeple
Hill®

ISBN-13: 978-0-373-87402-6
ISBN-10:   0-373-87402-2

MARRIED TO THE MOB

www.SteepleHill.com

Printed in U.S.A.

Daniel answered, "O king, live forever! My God sent his angel, and he shut the mouths of the lions. They have not hurt me, because I was found innocent in his sight.

—*Daniel* 6:21, 22

This book is dedicated to the caring and talented
physical therapists at Lancaster General Hospital's
Columbia Medical Center, without whose
help this book wouldn't have been written.

ONE

Somewhere in New Jersey

"What part of 'The mob's got a contract on you' do you not understand?"

Dan's whispered question didn't faze the stunning blonde at his side. She shrugged. "I understand you're trying to do your job, Mr. FBI Special Agent Maddox, but you should remember I've lived with these people all my life."

He went to press his point, but she cut him off.

"Do you really think they don't know where to find me?" She tossed her tawny mane. "They have more arms into more places, people and things than a family of octopuses…octopi?"

Dan looked around at the innocent bystanders, busy pretending not to listen. Why did he always get the nutcases? "How about this, Carlotta—"

"Hold it right there! Your memory's not so hot, is it? I've asked you and asked you *not* to call me that.

Carlie—*that's* what you want to call me. It's not so hard, is it? Try it, you might like it."

Her wink nearly sent his patience over the edge. "Do you ever take anything seriously?"

"Yes," she said, her eyes intent, her voice warm and vibrant. "I take God seriously. And then I leave the rest to Him."

Dan had heard this kind of crazy illogic before. David Latham, one of his closest friends and a fellow agent in the Philadelphia Organized Crime Unit, was a gung ho religion sellout. Then, after a recent case, his partner, J. Z. Prophet, went and married another one. To really throw him for a loop, J.Z. succumbed to the lure of false confidence in the same philosophical game of mirrors, and was now one of them.

"You go ahead and do that," Dan said, in a low voice. "But while you're in the Witness Protection Program, you better leave the driving to me—so to speak."

She rolled her large brown eyes. "Speaking of driving—"

"Would you *please* lower your voice? People are staring, and we don't want to draw attention to you."

Carlotta—Carlie—laughed. Here he was, trying to keep the crazy woman alive, and she laughed.

He tried again. "Don't laugh like that. Keep it quiet. I just told you we don't want to draw attention—"

"Just look—at where," she gasped between laughs, "we are. Then you tell me who's causing the commotion."

Dan pressed his forehead against the aggressively

pink door frame. "I know, I know, I know. But that's the whole point. Why did you feel the need to come—"

"Simple," she said. "I love nice nails, and mine looked like fence posts after a dust storm. So where did you want me to go? A drive-in lube shop?"

From the corner of his eye, Dan caught the fascinated stares of the nail techs, noses and mouths covered with baby-blue dust masks, and the dozen or so women in various stages of acquiring lethal prongs on the tips of their killer claws.

He took a deep breath. "Okay. Let's go. We've overstayed our questionable welcome."

"But I'm not done yet."

"Oh, yes you are." Dan grasped her upper arm and urged her toward the—what else?—pink door. "And I don't mean the paint on the nails either."

"But I have no color—"

"Believe me, you don't lack in that department." He glanced at the talons on her hands. "Even when your nails look like the glow-in-the-dark fake ones kids wear."

"How dare you? These are the finest acrylic—"

"You want to die for plastic nails?"

That finally made her pause. "Well, no. Of course I don't." She took a step toward the bubble-gum-colored front door. "But I'm not willing to live a shadow life either."

Dan took advantage of her forward motion and took hold of her hand. Carlie confounded him when she called out over her shoulder, "Bye, Dianna. Take care of little Davey, Sarah. Shonna, remember to tell your mom to try the echinacea for that cold. And Trish? Dump the jerk. He's not worth it—"

"What are you doing?" He turned to stare at her. "Who are all those women? How do you know them all?"

"I'm saying goodbye. Don't you do that when you leave?"

"Why did you come to a place where you've been before? Don't you realize that's the quickest way for your brother's pals to get you?"

"I didn't come back to where anyone knew me. This is the first time I've been here."

Why me? "So how do you know about the mother's cold or the other one's jerk?"

"I don't know. I said hi, and we got to talking. It's not just about the nails, you know."

"But you still risked your life for them."

"I told you I don't want to die for my nails."

He led them out of the shop and to his Bureau-issue car. "I'm glad you're not ready to die for plastic. And that shadow life you mentioned isn't a forever thing. All we need is a conviction on your husband's killers."

Carlie yanked her hand from his and stuck her fists on her slender hips. "And you really think that after my brother Tony, Joey-O, Larry Gemmelli and my dad are behind bars I'll be free to roam wherever I want?"

"Pretty much. At least, that's when my job ends, as far as you're concerned."

"Think again, Cop Boy. Larry's got more 'family' than Giant Stadium has seats. And they won't be too happy with me—they aren't already. Then there are all of good old Dad's zillion 'business associates.' Think they'll like visiting Dad at the pokey? Not hardly."

"What makes you think we won't get them all?"

"That's the dumbest thing you've said—"

A loud, appreciative wolf whistle cut her off and jerked him back to reality. "Come on. Get in the car. Before the next obnoxious idiot shoots a bullet instead of a whistle out his window."

She didn't budge. "Um…there's just one teeny, tiny, teensy-weensy problem here."

Yeah, her. "What's the problem now?"

"That's *your* assigned car, not mine. Do you figure you'll telepathetically drive mine back to the apartment?"

This was pathetic, all right. "Woman, you could drive a man right into a loony bin." He ran a hand through his hair. "No, I can't drive both cars back, nor can I come back by myself later. Go ahead. Drive yourself."

He looked around for his car's clone, but didn't see it anywhere. "So what'd you do with it?"

"I parked it out back, in the salon's lot. What'd you want me to do with it? Stick it in my pocket?"

Nothing fit in the pocket of her slim linen pants. "All right, Carlie. I'll walk you back to the car."

They began the trudge back toward Nail It. Dan looked up at the marquee, and shook his head. How much more ridiculous could a place get than to advertise its work with a gargantuan neon fingernail decorated with a hammer and—yes, of course—a nail, the pointed steel kind?

"While we're at it," Carlie said as they reached the

parking lot, "how about a better set of wheels? I mean, really. It barely moves. Do I look like I want to be a moving target in a poky-slow car?"

Against his better judgment, Dan looked at his gorgeous charge. From the top of her fabulous lioness's mane, to the satiny cream skin over model's features, to a curvy, feminine figure encased in the latest light green silk and old-gold linen, and all the way down to the feet in strappy, high-heeled green leather sandals— toenails coated with chipped polish—Carlotta Pappa- relli, mobster's widow, looked nothing like any target he'd ever seen.

And yet, at the same time, beautiful as she was, she was a target.

"Get real," he said. "A peacock car would be like waving a red cape at an angry bull. You need to blend in. That's the reason for the plain agency car, since there's not a lot we can do about you—unless you're ready for plastic surgery and a hair makeover."

She rolled her eyes—again. She was quite proficient at it, too. "Get over it, Danny Boy. I'm a blonde, not a boring bland, bland, bland, like the car."

That's for sure, that trouble-making corner of his head retorted. "Let's get something straight. You're no boring bland but a bottle blonde—"

"Ouch! That's not nice—"

"Neither are the guys after you." Would she ever get it? He went on as if she hadn't interrupted him. "And in the second place, no one calls me Danny Boy and lives."

"Wow! I never thought I'd ever see it—didn't know

you even had it. A sense of humor, that is. Is it an FBI requirement to be grim, gloomy and glum—*eeeeek!*"

She could've busted a window—maybe she did, but Dan didn't bother to check. He grabbed the shaking woman and shielded her body with his. That's how he approached the beige car.

He realized this might be Carlie's wake-up call. The formerly boring midsize model now sported a particularly realistic portrait of a massive rodent, and in case the observer didn't quite get the message, under the critter, it read *RAT*.

Dan pulled out his gun, held it in front as he approached the graffitied vehicle then gestured for Carlie to stay where she stood. When he circled the car, he noted an even more grisly message across the back window. The artist had detailed a skull and crossbones severed from a stick-figure skeleton. Again, the creative creep had titled his work *RAT*.

"Oh-oh-oh-oh-oh-oh-oh! Gross!"

Dan turned and saw Carlie's face glued to the passenger side window—the woman didn't listen worth a dime. Before he could yell at her—again—she resumed her wail.

"Yuck! There's a big, fat, repulsive rat in the front seat. Oh, would you look at that?" She looked at Dan and pointed. "Did you know their tails were *that* long? And hairless?"

"Yes—"

"And what's all that white fuzz all over the place—oh, that is so sick." She shuddered. "It's built itself a nest."

Dan shrugged. "Rats need homes. What can you do?"

"You are crazy." She headed back toward the front of the nail salon. "I'll have you know, Super-Duper Agent Daniel Maddox, *that's* no longer my car. As of right now. We can go back to yours, and you can have your pals from the Bureau pick up the rodent palace. I'm outta here."

Dan ran to her side, slid the gun back into the holster under his jacket, and reality slipped away. Slipped away? Yeah, right. It was zipping down the sanity highway, but what could he do? He'd been saddled with a beautiful but crazy witness.

She beat him to the car and stood at the passenger door. She crossed her arms. She tapped the toe of her stiletto-heeled sandal, as if she'd been there forever.

He unlocked the door. "Get in."

"Yes, Mr. Gracious."

Okay. It wasn't the nicest thing he'd ever done. But he was frustrated, they hadn't taught him how to deal with this kind of witness at Bureau training, much less law school, and she took too much pleasure driving him nuts. He slammed the door shut the minute her rear hit the seat.

And *he* had to keep her alive long enough to get convictions on her family and their dubious friends? He shook his head, rounded the vehicle, sat behind the wheel and peeled away, all without another word.

While he drove in silent mode, he continued to fume. Now he had to call Eliza, his supervising Special Agent. Not something a man—anyone—in his right mind would want to do. But from where he stood, he had no choice.

To be more accurate, Carlie had left him no choice.

He didn't know if he could keep her alive much longer. She refused to cooperate.

The next light turned against him. He sat and watched seconds crawl by. At his side, Carlie began to hum.

Dan hated humming.

And everyone had always called him laid-back. He scoffed. They oughta see the man he'd become post-Carlotta Papparelli.

She slanted him a look.

He ignored it.

The light turned green, so he drove on toward the safe house the Bureau had set up for Carlie in a massive, Lego block–type apartment complex.

Moments later he heard the faint *whee-uhn, whee-uhn, whee-uhn* of an emergency vehicle approaching from behind. He glanced in his rear-view mirror. The cherry light on the roof of the squad car strobed closer by the second. Dan pulled over to the shoulder.

"I hope no one's hurt," Carlie murmured.

Dan glanced her way. She'd closed her eyes, clasped her hands in her lap. Her expression, for once, was serious, intent. Somehow he knew she'd begun to pray.

Who for? The unknown—and only possibly injured—party?

Strange.

He merged back into the heavier-by-the-minute late-afternoon traffic. Carlie didn't speak. Neither did he.

Then sirens started up again. They approached from his right, so he eased up to the left shoulder. This time, an ambulance zipped up and rounded the corner. In less than three minutes, three more squad cars, an additional ambulance and two fire trucks raced by.

"Must be big," he murmured.

"I'm afraid so," Carlie answered, her voice softer and more serious than he'd heard it yet. She really wasn't that bad.

"I'm sorry."

She made a startled sound. "What for?"

"I acted like a jerk back there. I didn't need to slam the door on you."

"Thanks for the apology, but I'm not totally innocent either. I tend to have a smart mouth, and I gave you a pretty hard time. I know you're trying to do your job, and I understand you want to keep me alive, but I'm not used to all these restrictions. Besides, if the Lord wants me home at His side, then I'm ready to go."

A chill went through Dan. "Don't be so ready to croak, okay? You're very young. You've a long life ahead of you. By the way, how old *are* you? I mean, I have all that information in your case file, but I don't remember everything that's in it."

"I prefer to keep that piece of data private." A touch of humor came back into her voice.

"Not for long. When I get back to my place tonight, you'll be busted."

"I'll take what scrap of privacy I can get these days."

With an air of comfortable companionship between them, they turned the corner three blocks away from Carlie's apartment complex. As they approached, a nasty feeling took root in Dan's gut.

A hideous orange glow tinted the blue sky, and

clouds of smoke spread and hovered on the light wind. Right over the complex.

Dan slowed the car. At his side, Carlie caught her breath. His pulse pounded through him, throbbed in his temple.

Every one of his internal alarms detonated.

Which is what seemed to have happened to the structure, a detonation of some sort. All the emergency vehicles that had passed them no more than ten minutes earlier were lined along the backside of Carlie's apartment building. A HAZMAT team had joined the party, too.

That nasty feeling morphed into a ravening certainty. Still, he had to know. "You stay here," he said. "And I mean it, Carlie. Don't move."

She nodded, her eyes glued to the scene. Firefighters in their yellow suits ran around the trucks, some climbed the giant ladders, others helped people to the ambulances. Uniformed cops talked to a throng of civilians.

Dan approached an officer. "What happened?"

The woman turned to him and shrugged. "We're not sure. That's what we're trying to figure out."

A burly man in a white muscle undershirt and tan shorts walked up. "You wanna know what happened? I know what happened."

Officer Shenise Davis turned keen hazel eyes on the guy. "So tell me what happened, already."

"Easy there." The guy's bearded jaw pushed out. "Don't get your feathers all ruffled up, you know?" He shook his shaggy head. "Kids! Anyway, there's this blond broad who lives across from me, and either her gas line went nuts or something else did. All's I know is the place went *kaboom!* The whole building shook like one of them California earthquakes. Smoke started to stink up my place, and I opened the door. Well, the babe don't have much to go back home for—if she wasn't home, know what I mean?"

Dan knew. Too well.

The walking, talking wealth of information ran a massive paw through the wild thatch on his head. "Either the explosion busted her place to pieces, or else the fire ate it all up."

Although sure he already knew, Dan asked, "What floor was this?"

"Tenth, over in the middle section." He pointed an arm heavy with dark hair. "See? The ladder's up to the window to the right of the babe's place. Mrs. Schulz is seventy-five. Sure, she's got more vinegar to her than I got hair, but she can't go running or nothing like climb down on her own. I figure they're gonna have to carry her down…."

Dan gave what he hoped the officer and the verbose bear read as a nonchalant shrug, then walked back the excruciating distance between him and Carlie. He got in the car, turned the key, then shot her a sideways look.

"We're outta here. Your friends and family came calling, and they left you a calling card. Of the exploding kind."

"What do you mean?"

"Don't ask me where we're going, because I don't know. I have to call in, report this, check out what's available and then get you there. We can't stay here anymore. Someone bombed your apartment."

And then she threw Dan for a loop—again.

Carlie chuckled. "And you gave me grief about my nails. Just be glad I wasn't here. Face it, Danny Boy…er…Dan. I'd better get a manicure more often. It's good for my health. My nails—you know, the ones you said were going to get me killed—just saved my life."

TWO

Yes, she should be scared.

And yes, she was in serious danger.

But what could she do for herself? Nothing. So Carlie blocked out Dan's griping and turned to the Lord.

Father, I'm not so good at this yet, but I don't want to die. Don't get me wrong. If You want me, I'm there. But if it's not urgent, then I'd like to hang around here a little longer. The deal is, I don't know what to do, how to avoid Dad's and Tony's slimy friends. And Dan? Well, he tries, but there's a lot more of them than of us. So help us out here. Okay?

"You! Did you go deaf or something?"

Carlie shook herself. "No. I just had to…" He didn't share her new faith, but with this latest development… He'd asked. "I had to pray."

"Okay." He looked way uncomfortable. "Well. That's fine. Ah…we're going to have to pull over long enough for me to make some calls, get an idea what we should do next."

"Fine. What do you want from me?"

"Ah…nothing. I just figured you'd want to know why I was stopping when we need to get away ASAP."

Carlie peered at her companion, but couldn't read him, and she really did try. "Oh-kay, Mr. Secret Agent Man. I'll be right here, seat belt on, ready for takeoff whenever you're ready."

He gave her another of his exasperated looks. She had come to identify and catalog 37 flavors of weird looks Dan Maddox used on her—she would've preferred the ice cream. Pulling over to the side of the road wasn't the smartest thing to do. And yeah, yeah, she'd figured Dan as the Boy Scout–type right from the start. He'd never cell phone and drive. But the New Jersey Turnpike was no lonely country lane. Anyone could come along here and pop the two of them with the greatest of ease.

Ever since she'd helped Maryanne Wellborn, now Prophet, save her elderly father from dear brother Tony's murderous intents, Carlie's world had turned into a surreal series of images, each one weirder than the last. All because she'd agreed to testify against her father, her brother Tony and a bunch of their mob pals.

She'd also acquired her intense, good-looking blond shadow.

Carlie had never been so squeezed into a box. She'd called her father a tyrannical spoilsport during her high-school years. Then, after she married, Carlo gave her complete freedom—as long as she stayed out of his business.

That business, the same as her father's and brother's, was what landed her smack in the middle of this mess. She'd done everything she could during those years of marriage to ignore the signs, the same ones she'd ignored at home. What woman wants to admit her family, and the handsome, debonair older man her father insisted she marry, were all mobsters?

The driver's side door opened. "Okay," Dan said once behind the wheel again. "We're on our way."

"On our way where?"

"Some other place over in Pennsylvania."

"Could you be a little more specific? That covers a big chunk of ground, you know?"

He gave her another of those worried looks. "It's probably safer for you not to know too much about our plans."

"Oh, sure. I might telepathetically transmit the location to Dad's pals. Give me a break. What do you think I'm going to do? Hop out of the car—while it's zipping down a highway—flag down some unsuspecting soul, then run and tell on you?"

"It's *telepathically*, Carlie. And it's safer for you not to know too much in case someone takes me out and they snatch you."

"I like *telepathetically* better. And what you just said made no sense. If they snuff you—that's so cool! I feel like I'm reading the script for a TV cop show. Yeah, if they snuff you, don't you think they'll just grab me from the passenger seat? I'll be no more than a memory."

His knuckles went white on the steering wheel. "Sorry. You're right. I don't know what's wrong with me. I don't usually get this rattled on a case. I guess it doesn't help that I didn't get much sleep last night."

"Are you an insomniac?"

"No. Just working a tough case—you."

"Takes one to know one."

The corner of his mouth tipped up. "What is this? Elementary school?"

"Beats me. It's your game, remember? I'm just along 'cause you agency guys insisted I play. So where are you taking me? And I don't mean that little piece of ground out on the back forty of New Jersey some call Pennsylvania."

"Lancaster County."

She turned as far as the seatbelt let her to better look at him. "Oh! Can we stop at the outlets? Please. I love shopping there. You get the best deals on just about everything with a label."

Another weird look from Mr. Intense. "A bargain hunter mob wife? One who's become their number one target?"

"Hey! They can get me just as easily in a store as in this car. And just because I could get my hands on Carlo's and Daddy's money, doesn't mean I'm ready to pay more than I have to. That's just stupid."

"Okay. So you're a thrifty mob wife—"

"Widow, remember? The hit on Carlo is what started all this."

"You think I could forget?" He clamped his lips shut, swerved to avoid a maniac driver who cut them off from the right, then, once the nut was far enough away, changed lanes back to the right. Carlie clung to her seatbelt for dear life.

"By the way," he went on. "What was the deal with that empty coffin you guys shipped to Italy? He was supposed to be inside, but when Italian customs agents X-rayed the thing, it was empty as...well, you get my drift."

She sure did. He'd probably been about to say "your head" or pay her some other similar compliment, but she let him get away with the near-smear this time.

"There's no 'you guys,' Dan. I never knew what went on day-to-day, and I absolutely, positively had nothing to do with the funeral home, the funeral and why or for what reason they shipped off the empty casket for an Italian burial. I just knew Carlo'd died. His uncle Louie handled all the details."

He shot her a look Carlie didn't like. He didn't seem to believe half of what she said, but there was nothing she could do about it. The guy was the most suspicious critter she'd ever met.

He pushed the gas pedal, and the speed shoved her back into the seat. "What are you doing?"

"Getting off the Turnpike. This rush hour traffic is not my thing."

"But you live and work in Philly."

"Doesn't mean I have to like the traffic there."

Carlie studied his profile as they crossed the Delaware Memorial Bridge. So far, she hadn't found a thing Dan liked. What really threw her was that when he'd first been assigned to protect her, J. Z. Prophet, Dan's usual partner at the Bureau, had described her shadow as an easygoing, laid-back kind of guy.

This guy didn't have a laid-back hair on his blond head. And she was stuck with him. At least, until the trial was over and the verdict came in. After that...well, she didn't know what came after that, but she wasn't about to give it much thought. She still had to live long enough to get to "after that."

"Then allow me the pleasure to distract you from the horrors of after-work traffic," she said with a grin. "How about you tell me where you're taking me? I really, really want to know."

"We're going to a safe place just outside Bird-in-Hand."

"Huh?"

He shot her a smile. "So you don't know everything. Bird-in-Hand is a sleepy little town with *the* best Amish bakery and a huge quilting shop."

"*You* know about bakeries and quilt shops?"

"I'm a multifaceted kind of guy." He turned just enough for her to see his wink. "Actually, my mom's crazy about quilting, so she knows every one of those stores in the eastern half of Pennsylvania."

"So you're from that area."

"I grew up in a suburb of Harrisburg."

"Okay. Sounds good." By now he'd relaxed enough that his fingers didn't remind her of the color of over-cooked macaroni before the cheese was added any-more, a food group she now knew too much about thanks to her underground existence. "So how about you tell me where you're taking me—*exactly* where you're taking me? I mean, I have nothing against road trips, but really. This is just too weird."

"Curiosity is a dangerous thing, Carlie." He slowed down for a red light. "But I'll go ahead and tell you. My mom knows a Mennonite family who's willing to let us stay at their farm."

"Farm, huh?"

"Yes, the Millers own a dairy farm, and I remembered them when I tried to come up with a quiet, inconspicuous place to stash you. My mom and Mrs. Miller shop for their quilting supplies at the Bird-in-Hand store. Over the years they've become friends."

What was he getting them into? "The Mennonites, they're not the ones with the buggies and no electricity, are they?"

"No, those are Old Order Amish, but Mennonites are still very, very conservative."

She shrugged. "I'll figure it out as I go. I can handle anything as long as I get a decent night's sleep, a shower in the morning and a blow-dryer for my hair."

He squirmed in his seat, looked very, very uncomfortable. "We can do the sleep, and the shower shouldn't be a problem. But the blow-dryer might not be so easy. Because the women wear their hair twisted up in the small white *kapps,* I'm not sure the Millers own one, and yours is…"

Carlie's stomach sank. "Mine's a blob of melted plastic and a couple of blackened wires. So we need to look at this as a new life experience. Okay. I'm sure it'll come in handy someday."

From the way Dan's shoulders shook, she knew he was trying to hold in his laughter. At least she was good for comic relief. They had enough grim to survive. And Mennonites were Christians, so staying with the Millers couldn't be too bad.

They'd ditched the Pennsylvania Turnpike at around four o'clock. They pulled into the Miller farm at around six. The white farmhouse stood at the end of a long gravel drive. A huge oak tree spread its full, green branches in front of the home and shaded the wide porch. A big red barn flanked the rear of the house to the right. Various other smaller structures spread out toward the left rear. A bunch of black-and-white cows crowded each other on their way to what must have been dinner.

"Speaking of dinner," she said, "what are we doing for food?"

"Trust me," he answered with a smug smile.

"Oh, fine. Have it your way."

"I'm planning an experience you'll never forget."

Her stomach flipped. That easy smile made Dan look more human. And a million times more attractive. She wondered what he was like when not on the job.

"Come on," he said.

Carlie blinked. Saved by the bell…or something like that. She really couldn't afford to find her keeper appealing. So she'd better think about these people whose quiet life they were about to invade.

The woman who opened the door looked like a storybook grandma. This one, though, wore an unusual gray dress with sleeves that poufed a little on the shoulders then snugged down to just above the elbows. The dress made Carlie think of something one might have seen decades ago, if not way more than that. The plain top had a flat-over thingy that ended at the waistline. A skirt generous enough for the woman to do just about any kind of farm chore came down to the shin, where legs covered with dark cotton stockings led to old-fashioned black lace-up shoes.

Mrs. Miller shook her head when Dan told her a gas problem had left Carlie temporarily homeless. "So sorry to hear," she said, her voice spiced with a slight accent. "But please, make yourself welcome."

Carlie was charmed, but she felt like an impostor, lower than a slug. "Thank you so much, Mrs. Miller. I do appreciate your hospitality."

Their hostess smiled and gestured for them to follow her. "Come, come. Supper is served."

"Pay attention," Dan whispered close to her ear.

On their way to the kitchen, Carlie asked Mrs. Miller about the farm. She learned all kinds of details the woman gladly shared. And when they entered the enormous kitchen, Carlie understood what Dan had meant. A huge oak table filled the center of the room. Spread out over its surface was a feast, a banquet, a smorgasbord of sights and smells. Carlie's stomach growled.

Dan chuckled. "Told you."

"No, Mr. Close-mouthed Secret Agent, you did not. All you said was another of your enigmatic 'trust mes.' That didn't even give me a hint."

"You can't fault a guy for wanting to surprise a girl."

"You surprised me, all right."

"This is Richard." Mrs. Miller indicated the oldest boy. "Beside him is Jonas, then Ruth. On the other side, Rachel and Stephen…"

In minutes, Carlie asked and learned the children's

ages, where they went to school and their usual chores around the farm.

Finally, they joined the Millers, all seven of them, for the meal. Mr. Miller said grace in what sounded kind of like German, and after resounding amens, everyone dug in.

Evidently, Mrs. Maddox had let her friend know she'd soon have guests, and Mrs. Miller had put on what she called "a little more" into the pots and pans. To Carlie, it looked like she'd gone a whole lot further than that. A gentle prod with her fork broke the pot roast into tender morsels. Parsley and butter coated the potatoes, a colorful variety of homegrown veggies filled another third of her gargantuan plate, home-baked bread melted in her mouth, and cinnamon-dusted applesauce tasted more refreshing than Carlie remembered from her childhood.

"What do you think?" Dan asked.

"Wow! Nothing but wow."

Just when Carlie was sure she couldn't possibly swallow another mouthful, Mrs. Miller brought out two different pies. One was apple, and the other the well-known Pennsylvania Dutch shoofly pie.

"Which one?" their hostess asked.

"Oh, I'm going to try the shoofly," Carlie answered. "I've always wondered what it was like."

With her first bite, she fell in love, as she told her hostess, and thanked the kind woman for the best meal she'd eaten in years. Afterward, she insisted on helping Mrs. Miller and the girls in the kitchen, and when the last plate was put away, Carlie found herself more tired than she'd ever thought she could be. She yawned, and Dan caught her.

"Time to hit the hay," he said with a wink and a grin. "Say good night to our hosts, Carlie."

"Good night," she said like a dutiful child. But instead of heading upstairs, where she figured the bedrooms would be, Dan led her to the back door. "Where are we going?"

"I told you. You're going to hit the hay."

The glee in his face told Carlie more than she wanted to know. "You mean that literally, don't you?"

"Yup."

"How can you do that to me? I've been shot at, bombed—more than once, I might add—burned out of my apartment, and now you want me to sleep with the cows? You never told me about the perks of this deal, Danny Boy."

"Give me a chance to explain. Mrs. Miller didn't understand why I wanted you in one of the older out-buildings either. But think about it. If your family's pals follow us out here, and I'm not saying they will, but you never know, do you want to put the Millers at risk?"

"I never thought of that, and I should have." She sent a silent prayer heavenward. "Thanks, Dan. I'm so glad you did think it through."

Unless she was much mistaken, a hint of a blush warmed up the tan over his chiseled cheekbones. To her amazement, he looked embarrassed. By a simple thank-you. Go figure.

To defuse the awkward moment, she said, "Lead on,

fearless leader. Where do you want me? Roosting with the chickens?"

He pointed toward the left field. "There."

Oh, yeah. It was the one she'd feared he would choose. "Tell me why you decided we needed to occupy the frumpiest, dumpiest, most dilapidated pile of boards here?"

"Because the Millers are about to tear it down plus a couple of the other outbuildings, now that they put up the big red barn. If something happens while we're here, I don't want them to suffer any major loss."

Again his thoughtfulness surprised her—for the Millers, that is. "Let's go, then." She began to sing "Away in a Manger."

"You are just too much."

She snickered. "Too much what? Too much trouble? Too much fun? Too much of a good thing? Or maybe too much effort?"

"No way. That's the problem with you women. You lay traps for us guys to trip into. I'm not touching that one even if I'm drowning and it's the only thing that floats."

In a good mood, they reached the old structure. Dan held the wide, warped door open for Carlie. "Rich, the Millers' oldest son, brought out some pillows and bedding," he said. "You should be pretty comfortable."

She frowned. "What about you?"

"I'm keeping an eye out for trouble. Naps in the car aren't so bad."

"Great. Another guilt trip. I'm kinda tired of all the extra travel you're taking me on."

"Forget it. It's my job. I'm used to stakeouts."

She tilted her head and gave him a long look. "One of these days you're going to have to tell me all about being an FBI guy. It's not your everyday kind of job."

"Neither is being married to the mob. So once you tell me, I'll tell you."

Carlie held out her hand. "You got yourself a deal, Mr. Secret Agent Man."

He gave it a brief shake then let go as if burned. "Well. Ah…good night, Carlie."

"You, too."

She went inside, and on a pile of fresh-smelling hay against the rear wall Rich Miller had spread out the bedding. At one end, a pair of fluffy pillows were piled one on top of the other. All of a sudden, the strain of the recent upheavals overcame her.

Exhaustion claimed Carlie. She plopped down onto her makeshift bed, pulled the lightweight quilt over her shoulders, and dropped off faster than she thought possible.

A while later, she woke up. She had no idea what roused her, but she opened her eyes, her heart beating a frantic, furious pulse. Instead of her cozy quarters, she found herself in Dante's vision of Hades.

Tongues of flames licked toward the roof, the walls, her nest of hay. Smoke made it hard to see—worse, to breathe. The billows swirled before, beside, behind the flames.

"Oh, Father…dear God. Your will be done."

As she finished her scrap of prayer, she heard Dan's yell.

"Hang on, Carlie! I'm coming for you."

Everything went black.

THREE

Bit by bit, sound penetrated the thick, heavy darkness around Carlie. People jabbered, but she didn't understand a word. A rushing noise whooshed behind the chatter, and the smell of a barbecue gone bad stung her nose.

Then she remembered the fire. She remembered the meal, the Millers, the bombed apartment. Did Tony's slimy buddies get the farm, too?

She groaned. Everywhere she went, disaster and devastation followed.

A man called her name. He demanded that she breathe deeply. He commanded her to wake up. He ordered her not to die. "Come on, come on, come on!"

Carlie fought her heavy eyelids and tried to sit up.

No dice.

She needed someone to help her. The elephant who sat all over her body had to find a new seat, and the pins that held her eyes shut had to go.

But help didn't come. At least, not the kind she wanted. Instead, she was lifted upward, through the air, a frightening experience eased somewhat by the firm support at her back. A woman spoke, but Carlie still couldn't make out the words. Then she was poked, prodded, jostled, lifted, lowered, and then—finally— breathing wasn't quite so hard anymore.

A weird wail started up, and Carlie fought against the weight of her eyelids. After a superhuman effort, she got them pried apart and wished she hadn't. What she saw stunned her. Faces hovered just above her, weird gadgets hung beyond the faces, lights blinked, things clinked, and everything jerked and jolted to the tune of the ongoing wail.

"Carlie? Can you hear me, Carlie?"

She tried to answer, but her throat wouldn't work. She tried to nod, but her head wouldn't move—that scared her, so she tried to talk one more time.

"Don't," the female voice said. "Just blink if you can hear me. You have an oxygen mask over your nose and mouth, and that'll make speech difficult."

Oxygen mask! She blinked up a storm, but couldn't ask the million and one questions that buzzed in her head. What had happened between Dante's Inferno in a Mennonite barn and…where was she now? A hospital?

"Good," the woman said. "You can hear me. Let me explain a few things for you."

In a clear, soft voice, the woman told Carlie how Dan had axed a hole in the old, brittle wood walls of the small barn then dragged her out before the entire structure went up in flames. She'd passed out while in the burning building, and the Millers had called for the ambulance, which was now on its way to Lancaster

General Hospital. The EMT wound up her explanation by insisting that Carlie was lucky to be alive.

But Carlie didn't call it luck. She called it another of God's many mercies. She couldn't quite see a family like hers as any kind of luck, other than maybe the worst.

But where was Dan? Did he get hurt?

Carlie couldn't stand the thought of her shadow being harmed because of her. But she couldn't ask, and her head weighed about a ton. Her eyelids drooped again, and she slipped off for a nap.

Green and purple cows and orange and blue nails danced through her dreams.

"How much longer is she going to sleep?" Dan asked, frustrated.

Dr. Wong retained his calm. "We don't know, Agent Maddox. It depends on how she reacts to pain meds, plus a number of other variables."

"I have to get her out of here." Dan began to pace. "They nearly got her this time."

"This time?"

"That's why she's in the Witness Protection Program." When they'd first brought Carlie into the hospital, Dan had no alternative but to reveal his identity and their situation. It was the only way he could get adequate protection for his charge.

"Then I'd better not ask you more questions."

Relief felt good. "I appreciate that. And I appreciate the care you're taking with her."

"It's all in a day's work," the young doctor said with a grin. "I'll alert the rest of the staff. I'm sure they're dying to know about Carlie's vast and professionally serious extended family."

"Thanks." Dan hadn't known how he was going to disguise the crew his boss, Eliza, had sent. The doctor's understanding would go a long way in keeping things under some kind of control.

"But, Mr. Maddox?" the doctor said. "You yourself need to rest. You took in a big wallop of smoke, almost as much as Carlie did. And those burns of yours can get infected very easily."

Dan shrugged. "It's all in a day's work."

"Tripped up by my own words." Dr. Wong punctuated his words with a wry grin. He tapped his forehead in a salute, then turned and left the room.

Dan returned to his sentry post on the nasty green pleather chair next to Carlie's bed. But his patience wasn't much to write home about, and before too long, he paced again from the foot of the bed to the large window that looked out on congested traffic.

"Noooooooo!"

The ear-splitting scream shocked him still for a moment. Then he spun, ran to Carlie's side, and found her scooted up hard against the headboard, her legs bent at the knee, her medicine tree tipped partway over the bed.

Horror contorted her beautiful features, and the slight smudge of soot under her right eye, one the nurses missed when they'd cleaned her, added to the atypical, weirdly tough-girl look she now wore.

"Get out of here!" she yelled. With her non-IVed hand, she scrabbled through the pile of sheets and blanket at her side. It didn't take a genius to figure out what she wanted to find, who she wanted to summon.

"It's okay, Carlie. It's me, Dan Maddox. You're fine. The hospital and I are taking good care of you."

A bulldog expression replaced the horror on her face. "I don't know what your game is, bub, but you're not Dan Maddox. He has gorgeous blond hair. You don't have any."

Something in Dan leaped when she admired his hair. But it soon settled down thanks to reality. "Carlie, it *is* me. They shaved my head because so much of my hair got singed when I went after you in the barn."

She wrinkled her nose, and drew close. "You sound like Dan, but you look a little alien, kind of like that weird guy on the bottle, that Mr. Clean on TV commercials."

"Gee, thanks. I've always wanted to make a beautiful woman think of floor cleaner."

"Now I *know* you're not Dan Maddox. He'd never tell me I'm beautiful. He'd call me trouble, a pain, crazy and who knows how many other snotty names."

What could he tell her? That he had to force himself to think of her along those "snotty" lines to keep him from thinking of her as the drop-dead gorgeous woman she really was? That he didn't want to admit her quirky sense of humor made it tough for him to keep from laughing? That he was scared to death he might fall for her over the duration of his assignment?

Not in this lifetime.

"I'm sorry you think I'm snotty, but you are a

handful," is what he went with. "And you don't make my job—keeping you alive—any easier."

"Oh." She seemed to melt into her pillow. "You are Dan after all. Well, I guess that's good. You really look scary, though. Wouldn't want to bump into you in a dark alley."

"Maybe that'll help us. Just think. Maybe I'll scare your brother's buddies away."

She snorted. "That's not even funny. They're pretty determined." She settled down under her blanket again. "So what's our next move?"

"It's not all sewn up yet, but one thing's for sure. We're leaving the mid-Atlantic area ASAP. They got your apartment, and they followed us to the Millers' place."

Before Carlie had a chance to comment, a knock at the door drew their attention. Dan slipped his hand inside his jacket then nodded for her to answer.

He never would have guessed the identity of her visitor. Fourteen-year-old Jonas Miller walked in, his steps hesitant, his face flushed, his old-fashioned button-down shirt and dark navy pants an odd contrast to his youth.

"Jonas!" she exclaimed. "How are you? Do your parents know you're here?"

Pure misery filled his adolescent face. "*Ja*. They know. They made me come. They even brought me."

She blinked. "I see. And why would that be?"

The boy looked down at his feet and mumbled something Dan didn't catch. Obviously, neither did Carlie, since she asked him to repeat himself.

"I'm sorry, miss. I didn't mean for this to happen."

Carlie looked more puzzled than ever, but her voice

came out soft, gentle, caring. "What are you sorry about, Jonas? What is the 'this' that happened?"

He shrugged. "Didn't mean for the old barn to burn."

"And that means...?"

"That it was all my fault." Jonas looked ready to cry. "I—I know it was wrong, but the guys are always mocking me, so I figured I'd better practice for the next time after school."

Dan knew what was up, but Jonas had to do this on his own.

"What were you practicing?" Carlie asked.

Jonas shifted his weight from foot to foot. He shoved his hands in his pockets. Then he seemed to come to a decision, squared his shoulders and stared straight at Carlie.

"I don't want to choke when I smoke again!"

Carlie's reaction was a quick blink. Dan had to fight the laugh on its way out. Then his mob widow surprised him—again.

"That's the easiest thing," she told Jonas. "All you have to do is *not* smoke. You'll never choke that way. And those 'friends' will be the ones to worry about lung cancer and emphysema while you're still healthy as a horse. You'll have the last word."

"But these guys already tease me because...well, I...I..."

The poor kid's face turned redder than pizza sauce.

He shrugged. "I get good grades. It's not so hard. I just go to class, do the homework, and that's it. But they think I'm some kind of sissy."

"Jonas, my man," Carlie said, a smile on her lips.

"Come on over here. Have a seat in Dr. Carlie's office. You and I need to have us a chat."

Dan's admiration grew as each one of the next fifteen minutes went by. With her sense of humor and brilliant smiles, Carlie soon had the teen laughing with her. By the time she was done, Dan knew Jonas Miller would never pick up another cigarette. And he genuinely regretted the fire he'd caused. Then Carlie threw him for a loop.

She held her hand out to Jonas and invited him to join her in prayer. For some strange reason, their earnest expressions did something to him. He didn't back off as he normally would have, but instead he stayed and watched them, their heads close, their hands clasped, their voices low and intense.

An odd pang hit him, a sudden loneliness, nothing he'd experienced before, something he hoped never hit him again. It was a restless sensation, an urge for some unknown something, a sense of need.

After they said amen, Jonas headed for the door. "Bye, Miss Carlie."

"Now you just wait one cotton pickin' minute there, Jonas Miller." Carlie's fake scolding dripped with her trademark humor. "You don't think you can leave here without giving me a hug, do you?"

Dan watched the boy, one whose background inspired reserve, bend down to Carlie and give her the hug she'd asked for. It was an awkward, stiff hug, but a hug is a hug is a hug.

Amazing.

A nurse came into the room as Jonas left and she

shooed Dan away. She insisted he had to go so she could take Carlie's vital signs. He left, went to the snack shop downstairs, and bought himself a bucket of coffee and a gooey sticky bun. Of course, as soon as he bit into the pastry, his cell phone rang.

"Yeah," he mumbled around the mouthful of delicious dough.

"How's it going?" asked his partner, J. Z. Prophet.

"If I said bad to worse, it wouldn't begin to give you a clue."

"What's the deal? The family's after you again?"

"They never stopped." Dan gave J.Z. a brief rundown of the latest events, even told his partner about Jonas's ill-fated attempt at being cool. That made them both laugh, but didn't ease their concern.

"You know what's got to happen, don't you?" J.Z. asked.

"Yeah. We've got to hit the road again. I'm just waiting for Eliza to let me in on the secret of our destination."

"And she's no more cooperative than usual."

"You got it."

"Well, Maryanne and I will keep you both in our prayers. Be safe."

The prayer bit made Dan squirm on his stool. He ignored that statement, and said, "You, too."

He hurried to finish his pastry and the transfusion of caffeine. He had to get back to Carlie. Who knew what kind of trouble she'd kicked up by now? The woman needed a keeper, and unfortunately, the Bureau had picked him for the job.

The second he stepped into the elevator, his cell

phone rang again. This time, the caller wasn't quite as welcome as his previous one.

"Yes, Eliza. Do you have instructions for me?"

In brief, his boss gave him a laundry list of steps to follow. When she finally disclosed their ultimate destination, Dan couldn't stop his groan.

"You've got to be kidding, Eliza. That's inhuman."

"Live with it, Maddox. It's the best solution for a difficult situation. Or to be more accurate, the best solution for a difficult witness."

He didn't much care to hear his snippy boss refer to Carlie that way; it was different when he did it. He knew Carlie, while Eliza had just met her once or twice during the investigation into Carlo Papparelli's murder.

"Fine," he said. "We'll take off as soon as the doctors let her go."

"You might not want to wait that long, Agent Maddox. I won't tell you how to do your job, even though I can, and you know it, but don't think time is on your side."

The elevator door opened just as Dr. Wong walked out of Carlie's room. "I hear you loud and clear, Eliza. And now I have to go meet with Carlie's doctor. I'll let you know as soon as we hit the road."

Dan hurried to catch up with the doctor. He explained the need for speed, the urgency of the situation.

But Dr. Wong refused to commit. "I'll discharge her as soon as she's ready to go."

He wouldn't budge from that stance, no matter what Dan said. So, more frustrated than ever, he retreated to Carlie's room.

"Hey, Sunshine," she called when he walked in. "What's with the joy and happiness?"

That was all he needed: Carlie in one of her more outrageous moods. How was he going to break the news to her?

"How are you feeling?" he asked.

"I'm a lot better. But it still feels like I breathed in a bunch of mascara brushes."

Mascara brushes? "Then I hope you cough out the little porcupines faster than you breathed them in."

"What do you mean?"

"I mean that you're going to have to feel well enough to sneak out of here sometime tomorrow. We have to get going while we still can."

Her eyes widened, and she swallowed hard. "Where are we going? Or can't you say?"

"I shouldn't say anything, but I know how hard this has been on you. Prepare yourself. We're headed for the steam bath better known as Florida in August."

Once again, Carlie took his words and turned them upside down. "Really?" she asked, excitement in her voice. "I've always wanted to go to Florida! Promise me one thing."

"I'm not promising anything. Tell me what you want, and I'll tell you whether we can work it out."

She sat up and crossed her arms. "Work it out, nothing. You owe me, Secret Agent Man. You wouldn't take me shopping at the outlets, so now you have to take me to see the Mouse. We, Danny Boy, are going to Disney World."

Dan had the sinking feeling he'd lost control of his

assignment. And the loss was all because of a beautiful blonde, her killer smile and his growing desire to please her.

He was in trouble. And it had nothing to do with the mob.

It was the mob widow who posed the danger, to his health.

His heart's health.

FOUR

That bruise on Carlie's forehead was going to drive him nuts. How long did bruises last, anyway?

Against his better judgment, he stole another glance across the width of the front seat of his Bureau car.

He had to face the truth. Her beauty exerted a pull on him. It was shallow of him, but with a woman as attractive as Carlie Papparelli, a man would have to be totally blind not to feel it.

He wasn't blind.

The small bruise over her left eyebrow stood out from the near-perfect background of her looks and underscored her vulnerability. It made him more aware than ever that her life—literally—was in his hands. He'd never shied away from responsibility, and he wasn't about to start now, but for some reason this assignment weighed more heavily on him than most others did.

He almost couldn't recognize himself.

Everyone he knew commented on his easygoing nature, his lighthearted view of the world, his ability to cope in tough circumstances with ease and poise. That all changed the day he'd met the mobster's widow.

He didn't like it. Not one bit.

Another glance.

Carlie had closed her eyes, leaned her head against the window and appeared to nap. The slightest hint of a smile curved her lips, and her peaceful expression nearly stole Dan's breath away. How could she stay so calm?

Mobsters wanted to make mincemeat out of her, yet she still slept with the trust of a child.

Maybe she did trust him. He hoped so, because otherwise their circumstances would be grimmer than even he thought them to be. He knew his job; he had an excellent track record with the Bureau. He'd yet to lose a single witness under his care.

One more look at her reminded him of the scale of his task.

He usually handled mousy paper-pushers who'd blown the whistle on crooked colleagues. He'd never had to worry about making the subjects of those assignments inconspicuous; they *were* inconspicuous. But Carlie?

He needed someone to show him how to turn a stunning Cinderella back into a frumpy maid. He didn't have a magic slipper to take from her foot.

The thought of her footgear made him smile. Carlie struck him as a firm supporter of "the more, the merrier" approach. That is, when it came to her heels. He'd never seen anyone handle stilettos, even while wearing jeans, quite as expertly as Carlie Papparelli did. The most irritating part? She looked great while doing so.

He chuckled. She'd better hope they didn't have to

hoof it to safety any time soon, because if they did, she'd be in major trouble. Those spikes weren't made for running.

When he realized how indulgent his thoughts were, he forced his attention to the matter at hand. He couldn't afford to expend many warm and fuzzy thoughts on Carlie as a person. That would spell danger.

So he drove on in silence.

She slept on.

"Hey!" she said about two hours later. "How about we hit a fast food joint or something? It's way past time for me to use the little girls' room."

"And here I thought you just loved the little toys."

"Watch it, Secret Agent Man. If I get a squirt gun, you're in trouble."

Dan cringed when, as they walked into the burger place, every head turned their way. All its patrons stared at Carlie, who, oblivious of the attention, headed for the ladies' room.

Yeah, he had trouble on his hands, all right. The biggest part of that trouble was to convince Carlie that something had to be done about her looks.

"Aw, come on," she wheedled moments later. "Why can't we eat at least one meal a day at a table? I'm really tired of squeezing stuff out of foil packets and decorating my clothes with it because you hit yet another bump."

He almost broke. Almost.

"Be glad that's the only kind of bump we've hit on the road to a long and healthy future for you. Those bombs and bullets weren't figments of our imaginations."

She shuddered, and an infinitesimal pang of guilt hit him. But then, in a subsequent moment of reason, he banished the pang to where it belonged: far, far away from his thoughts.

"I intend to get you to that witness stand in one piece. If that means you're going to wear a mustard-ketchup-and-barbecue-sauce tie-dye job, then you'd better get yourself a new perspective on stains."

She rolled her eyes, grabbed her bagged meal, turned away, and *click-click-clicked* her way to the door. There she paused to give him a glare. "So, Danny Boy, are you just going to stand there? If my memory serves me right, you're the one who finished reading me the riot act about the dangers of exposure not two seconds ago."

He shook his head and followed.

Outside, he yielded just a bit. They ate in the parked car. In silence.

When Carlie was done, she turned to face him. "How long is it going to take you to get me to Florida? All I know is that we've been driving for ages, and I don't see any sand or palm trees yet."

"That's because it takes more than a couple of hours to drive from Pennsylvania to Florida. Especially if we want to make sure none of your family's friends are on our tail."

She sighed. "So how much longer do you want us to live out of your car?"

"As long as it takes." He ran a hand through his hair. "Actually, I don't think it'll be more than three or four days."

"Are you kidding?"

The horror on her face almost made him laugh. He controlled the urge. "Okay, okay. Tell you what. We'll take the scenic, tourist route, and go through quaint little towns with well-maintained Victorian cottages. That way you'll be able to enjoy the picturesque views."

"How about that nice, quiet place in Florida you told me about? I'm looking forward to a regular home—at least, for a while."

He could understand how she felt. He'd worked for the Bureau long enough that he'd come to hate the anonymity of hotel rooms. He also hated to sleep in his car during a stakeout. His nomadic lifestyle got to him at times, even though it came as a result of his chosen career. Carlie hadn't chosen any of this.

"Look, I know you're in a rotten situation," he said, his tone conciliatory. "But it would be even more rotten if anything happened to you—"

"Get real! What you mean is that it would be rotten if they whacked me. You'd lose your prime witness, and your oh-so-important case would go down the toilet. There's nothing about *me* in your plan."

"It's all about you, Carlie. I don't want to see you dead. I joined the Bureau to protect my country and its people. Last time I checked, you were a citizen. I don't think anything's changed that."

"There you go again. I'm a citizen." She crossed her arms. "That's garbage. I know what I'm facing, and I still have an identity. There is still life ahead of me. Spending what's left locked inside this rolling tin can—" she pounded the car door "—is not what I'm ready to do."

His frustration reached the boiling point. "Well then, I guess that choice is out of your hands. You may have some weird kind of death wish, but I'm not going to play. Buckle up. We're out of here."

She yanked the seat belt down to the latch, and once he heard it click, he turned the key in the ignition.

He pulled to the parking lot exit then waited for traffic—a single school bus full of kindergarteners.

"I don't suppose you're going to tell me where we're headed next," she said.

"You suppose right. Your best plan is to get some more of that beauty sleep you've been catching up on. Who knows what's going to happen even ten minutes from now."

They drove again in that uneasy quiet he'd come to expect. How could he tell her he was winging it? That he didn't have a plan besides making sure no one followed? That wouldn't reassure her. It didn't make him feel all that great either, but under the circumstances, it was the best he could do.

When he couldn't stand the stony look on her face and her shrieking silence for another minute, he turned on the radio. Although he'd never gotten into the sports-over-the-radio deal—no visuals—he found a station that offered kick-by-kick coverage of a soccer game somewhere in the Hispanic world. Even the loud, heartbeat-like drumming in the background was better than the thick, uneasy stillness.

The hysterical cries of *"Gol, gol, gol"* when either team scored provided a weird kind of punctuation for the afternoon. When the game ended, he frantically searched for a classical music station.

Then the sun finally began its descent toward the horizon. That simple reality forced him to face the need to come up with another meal option and overnight choice. He couldn't drive all night after driving all day. He'd only snagged about three hours' sleep the night before. The way he saw it, he had no choice but to find an out-of-the-way motel, nothing like the famous chains that everyone recognized.

"Um…"

Carlie's murmur caught his otherwise-engaged attention. "What's up?"

"You've worn this fierce expression for hours now. Tell me it has something to do with my next meal and a place to take a hot shower."

He chuckled. "Believe it or not, that's exactly what's been on my mind."

"How so?"

"More than food, we need to find a safe place to stay the night. I have to catch some sleep so I can continue driving—"

"I've told you I'm a great driver, but you just won't share. You could have taken a nap anytime today."

"You're getting over a concussion. How can you drive long distance?" He gave her an exasperated glare. "I'd rather drive till I drop than nap and find myself wrapped around the nearest lamppost. Your rattled brain could wig out on us anytime."

"I'd rather trust my rattled brain than ride next to a guy who's sleep deprived. Doctors have proved that a sleep-deprived brain behind the wheel is the equivalent of an intoxicated brain."

He sighed. "We're not going to discuss the merits of medical studies. We're going to focus on finding a motel."

"Fine. I know we've passed a couple of cute ones along the way. I just hope we haven't run out of luck on that regard—"

"Nope. Look to your right. And the best part about it is that across the road there's a—"

"Wow! A real diner. The kind with the shiny metal building! I didn't know those still existed."

He clicked on his turn signal. "You never know what you'll find along a back road. There are still diners in Pennsylvania. I suppose North Carolina's the same."

"So that's where we are." She grinned. "You let the cat out of the bag. Uh-oh! Carlie now knows where she is!"

Dan had never rolled his eyes this much in his whole life. It was contagious—he'd caught it from her. "I'm going to trust you to keep your mouth full of food. That way you won't blab. Then sleep should do the trick for a few hours overnight. After that, I'll have you so lost, you won't know what hit you."

"I'm going to assume you think you're being cute."

"No. Just dealing with you the best I can."

"Let's eat."

"Well, well, well," Dan said as he parked in the diner's lot. "We have to mark this moment. Our first agreement so far! I hope it's a sign of more harmony to come."

The truce of sorts lasted through dinner. Carlie oohed and aahed over meatloaf, mashed potatoes and gravy, creamed corn, buttered peas and apple pie with vanilla ice cream. Dan had to agree that the meal came close to Mrs. Miller's supper. And he did love comfort food.

Then they drove across the street. In the motel's tiny lobby, they both endured the owner's scrutiny. After all, how many couples their age asked for separate rooms in an out-of-the-way place? The discomfort, however, was nothing compared to what he'd feel if Carlie were harmed.

Once in his room, he enjoyed every second of a quick shower. And then he collapsed on the surprisingly welcoming bed.

Nothing woke him until the alarm rang. Tendrils of sunlight slipped around the blue and gold curtains on the window.

He dressed, threw his few belongings in the duffel bag he always kept in the trunk of his Bureau-issue car, and headed out. He fully intended to knock on Carlie's door, but the sound of laughter out in the parking lot derailed his intentions.

What he saw left him stumped. Three children, all of whom appeared to be under the age of ten, two girls and a toddler boy, had drawn a chalk hopscotch on the asphalt. The oldest girl threw a round rock to one of the squares then hopped one-legged in the traditional steps of the game.

But the kids weren't the ones who'd caught his attention. The woman cheering the girl, however, was. Carlie had pulled her long, blond mane into a ponytail, and despite her high heels, looked more like a young babysitter than the widow of a shady character.

Her eyes sparkled in the morning sunshine; her cheeks wore a soft rose tint; her voice rang with enthusiasm; her slim body looked ready to take on the game—and win.

There was something about that woman…something that drew him and scared him in equal measure. If he were a smart man, he'd listen to his fearful side. He had to constantly remind himself that they weren't on vacation, that she had the mob on her tail, that she would have died had the Bureau not put her into the Witness Protection Program.

"Morning!"

Her radiant grin hit him square in the gut and stunned him for a moment. She took his brief silence and continued.

"Drop that bag and come join us. We're having *fun!*"

Fun? They were supposed to be on the run. Once again, Carlie seemed able to find something to appreciate in even the direst situations. He didn't know another woman who would cope as well.

"Don't be a party-pooper!" The teasing look on her face tugged at him. "Come on, Danny Boy, be a sport."

The three little ones stared at him in fascination. The younger girl took a step forward. "Yeah, mister. You can play with us. It's not so hard. I'll show you."

A small hand reached out for him. A car drove down the road past the motel. His professionalism returned with a vengeance, but he found himself unable to deny the child…or the woman.

"One time," he said, dropping his bag. "Only one time, okay?"

The kids clapped.

Carlie murmured, "Thanks."

He hopped, and memories of his childhood flooded him. It had been a long time since he'd thought of things like hopscotch on a summer morning. The games he'd played recently involved expensive equipment and far-flung locales. He enjoyed golf and tennis, but the simple pleasure of tossing a rock and bounding from square to square on one leg touched a different corner of his being.

Bang!

His instincts took over at the blast. He reached behind his back and drew his pistol.

"Run!" he yelled, and aimed.

But no one moved. The kids stared at him, their eyes wide open, their mouths forming perfect *O*s. Carlie also stared, but her stare came full of fascinated horror.

"What are you waiting for?" he cried. "Run for cover."

She dropped to the children's level and opened her arms. The boy toddled to her. She held the little guy close, murmured something soothing to the girls and then gave him the glare he'd come to expect from her.

"You owe them an apology," she said, her voice quiet. "You've scared them for no reason."

"No reason?" He shook his head and pointed to the plain car with his weapon. "Get in there before they come back for another try."

Carlie shook her head. Her look turned pitying. "Have you lost all touch with reality? Is that what your job does to you?"

"Reality, lady, is that you've got a bull's eye on your back."

"Reality, Dan, is that you overreacted to a car's backfire."

"What?"

"Dan…" She patted the boy then stood and approached, exasperated. "That old truck backfired when the driver pulled into the diner while we played, and it did the same thing a minute ago after the guy finished his breakfast or cup of coffee. Get real. We're in the middle of nowhere. My family's not about to show up here. Put that thing away, okay?"

He scanned the road, and when he saw nothing to arouse his suspicions, he realized how ridiculous he looked. Not to mention how frightening he appeared to three little kids. His outstretched arm suddenly weighed more than the average tree trunk, and his face heated up.

"Ah…well, if you're sure that was a truck…"

"Listen up, Secret Agent Man, we'd better get out of here before the motel owners come out, see you in spook mode and call the cops. That wouldn't help our cause any, would it?"

With one quick move, he shoved his gun into his waistband and grabbed his duffel bag. "You're right. Let's go."

She grinned. "Can I have that in writing? That 'you're right' thing? It's the first time. We need to mark the event."

He chuckled. Against his better judgment. But instead of commenting, he unlocked the car, threw his bag into the back seat, placed the gun on the console, where he always kept it while driving on assignment, and then turned to the kids.

"Sorry, guys. I figured we could maybe play 'cops and robbers,' but Carlie is right. We have to go. Maybe next time we'll play some more."

He slid behind the steering wheel and waited for Carlie to buckle up. Through the windshield, he watched the little boy run to his oldest sister and bury his face in her belly, while the younger girl reached out and patted him on the back. The air of vulnerable innocence hit him hard.

"Do you have any idea how stupid that stunt was?" he asked, barely leashing his anger.

"What stunt? All I did was play with a couple of kids."

"Exactly. In an open parking lot, with no protection, in full view of the road. You know we're being followed, yet you just hopped around out there."

"But nothing happened—"

"They could've picked you off!"

"That could happen any time, Dan. I have to continue to live."

"And how about innocent bystanders? Like the kids? Do you think your brother's pals would spare that little boy? Or the girls? Not if they thought those children could identify them."

Carlie gasped. Out the corner of his eye he caught her expression. Shock etched her face. All color drained from her cheeks, the sparkle left her eyes. She began to shake.

"Oh, Lord Jesus," she murmured. "Forgive me."

On the tail of her prayer, the tears began to fall. They didn't come as a surprise. What stunned Dan was his pain at every drop that rolled down Carlie's cheeks.

He didn't want this.

He didn't want to be this vulnerable—to her.

But he was.

He wanted to wrap his arms around her, hold her until the last tear dried, to promise her she'd be safe, that he'd make sure of that. But he couldn't do that, none of it.

So instead he continued to drive, his feelings in a kind of tangle he'd never experienced before.

FIVE

Dan had never felt so incompetent in his life. Up till now, he'd always been confident in his abilities, but now, when faced with Carlie's contrite misery, he had no idea how to proceed. Was there anything he could do? Could he offer comfort? How?

And her faith…how did he deal with that?

That faith seemed to be her greatest source of strength, of…well, yes, comfort. She'd kept her head down while she wept, and although he didn't hear any proof of it, he knew she was deep in prayer. Any word he might offer seemed inadequate in this circumstance.

What did he know about faith?

Nothing.

All he had on which to put his trust was his training, experience and instincts. He couldn't see the point of relying on some vague being out there somewhere.

Her words broke into his thoughts. "I can't begin to tell you how sorry I am," she said, her voice soft and sad.

He tightened his hold on the steering wheel. "I know that. But you can't go on beating yourself up about it.

What's done is done, and you have to look at the upside. No one was hurt."

"Of course, I see that. What bugs me most is my thoughtless behavior. I'd rather think I'm more aware of what's happening around me. Oblivion isn't a good thing—at least, not in my case."

He kept his eyes on the road, even though everything inside him urged him to look her way. "If it made you more aware of reality, then in the end, it was worth it."

"But those kids…"

The shudder that racked her reminded him again of her extreme vulnerability. He reached out to place a hand on her forearm. "Carlie, forgive yourself. You made a mistake. You're human. We all make mistakes."

"That's going to be tough," she said. "I know God forgives me, but I'm not nearly strong or wise enough to see how I can forgive myself."

Now what did he say? Where was J.Z. when he most needed the guy? Since nothing came to him, Dan offered a soft, wordless, hopefully sympathetic murmur, and continued to drive.

After a while, she turned toward him. "You know, I'm not afraid for myself. I'm serious, I don't want to die, but more than what I want, I'm interested in what God wants. If He wants me to go home to His side, then I'm ready to go."

She'd done it again. What could he say to that? He didn't have that kind of belief.

So he just said what came to his mind. "I can't quite get my head around that attitude of yours. Don't get me wrong. I'm familiar with it. J.Z. and David, another agent at the Bureau, believe as you do. But I...I don't get it."

She stared at him for a moment, her gaze piercing and, he suspected, perceptive. He wriggled in his seat.

"I was in that place not so long ago," she said. "And it wasn't all that great an address. The loneliness hurt more than any other pain I've known."

"But I'm not lonely," he argued. "I've got friends—David and J.Z., for instance—and I'm always surrounded by people, suspects and colleagues."

Her smile spoke of secrets. "Um-hmm, I know what you mean. But what happens when you go to bed at night, when you close the door to all those 'friends and colleagues,' when it's just you in the dark?"

The question hit a private corner of his heart. He shrugged, somewhat defensive. "I'm like everyone else. We're all alone when you strip away the outside world."

"Oh, no. We're not all alike." This time she reached out, put her hand on his shoulder. "Not if we realize we don't have to be alone."

"If you're suggesting marriage or a dog, you might as well forget it."

"Don't be so blind on purpose." She shook her head. "You know where I'm going, and I won't let you pull that kind of dumb act. You have Christian friends. You know they're where I am on this. We're not alone in the dark."

"Now you're going to tell me I have to come to Jesus, to be born again, to fall on my knees, a broken-down man."

"If you would just cut out the sarcasm, maybe then we'd get somewhere."

"Don't you understand?" He spared her a sideways glance; her irritation made him even more uncomfortable, more resistant, more determined to get his point across. "There's nothing out there for me to see, to cling to when the loneliness hits."

Another shake of her head, this one accompanied with a look filled with pity. "Have you even tried? Have you ever reached out to God, to see if He did or didn't answer?"

"Of course not. I'd feel ridiculous talking to something I couldn't see or feel."

She chuckled. "That, Danny Boy, is what's called faith. We reach out and trust that something we can't see or feel. And that's exactly when God comes and meets us, at our most fragile moment, when we have no safety net under us."

He shrugged. "I'm not ready to take that fall."

"He won't let you fall. God will catch you in the palm of His hand, and never let you go."

"It must be nice to have that kind of image to hold on to." Somewhere inside him, an even greater gaping hole than that of the private loneliness made its presence known. "I'll admit I sort of wish I could believe. And I get what makes you tick these days. But I can't join you on this. I can only count on myself."

"And you think you can…oh, let's say, go into the lion's den, armed only with your self-reliance and your gun, and beat my family and all their connections? One other Daniel didn't think that was so smart."

He blushed. "Well, if you put it that way, it does sound kind of arrogant."

"Yep. That's just a teeny-tiny little bit like seeing yourself as equal to God."

"Hey, I never said that."

"No, but that's the attitude that, like you said, makes you tick."

His squirming got worse. He'd never thought of himself as arrogant, just a confident, self-sufficient man. "Look, all I know is that the federal government spent a bundle to train me. I'm an expert at what I do, and I'm highly motivated. Not only is success the goal in the job I love, but I'm personally sold out here, in your case."

"What do you mean?"

"I owe you for what you did. You saved J.Z.'s wife—my partner's future wife back then. That means a lot to me."

"So you only see me as a job, a duty to repay a debt."

"A crucial job, one that demands commitment at a higher level than most, and it's an obligation I'll gladly undertake, no matter how great the responsibility. After all, it's in my hands, my alertness, my response to danger, whether you live or die."

"Phew! Boy, am I glad I'm not you!"

"Huh?"

"Sure. That's just a little bit pompous, you know— stuffy and stuck on yourself. You've set yourself up for a fall—that attitude is going to smack you right between the eyes one of these days. It'll knock you down on your behind, too. I just hope you don't take some innocent with you when the time comes."

"That's not what I—"

"Give it up, Dan."

His eyebrows rose. He'd never heard her so serious or so persistent. All her kidding had vanished. He wished he weren't driving; he'd love to watch the play of expression over her beautiful face.

She went on. "Whether you can see it or not, you've set yourself up at a level where only God can be. You don't determine whether I or anyone else lives, not even you. God's the One who has, not just our hairs counted, but the minutes and seconds of our life under control. I'd rather trust in Him than in a supercop who thinks so much of himself."

What could he say to that? She'd slammed him a low blow. He didn't have some weird complex…did he? He just knew what he knew, his job, his training. He was a self-assured man who knew himself and where he wanted to go in life.

Right?

She wasn't right.

Was she?

There hadn't been much more to discuss after that heavy talk about faith, so neither one had said another word. The radio had filled the car's interior with a hodge-podge of music styles. The farther they drove, the more stations changed. Swing switched to rock to jazz to classical to political commentary. That last didn't go on for long; either Carlie or Dan changed the channel as soon as the endless partisan arguments popped up.

At least they agreed on one thing. Actually, they also agreed on food. Dan admired the way Carlie didn't pull the I-eat-like-a-bird routine. She had a healthy appetite, and she didn't hide her appreciation of her meals. How she stayed slim eating that way, he didn't know.

It was somewhere between North and South Carolina that he noticed the blue Honda behind them. He remembered spotting it the last time he took a turn. He spat out a choked sound.

How could he have let this happen? Since when did he let his mind wander? And to the point of distracting his attention.

To check things out, he slowed down and gestured out his window. "Hey, Carlie. Take a look at that old farmhouse. It doesn't get more picturesque than that."

The Honda slowed down.

Carlie shot him a bewildered look. "Are you trying to tell me you want me to play tourist now? What's up, Danny Boy?"

He pressed the pedal. "You wanted more than just to get from point A to point B, didn't you? There!" He made a major production of it as he pointed to a cow. "That's as rustic Americana as can be."

The Honda sped up.

Carlie stuck a finger in her ear then shook it. "I must be hearing things. You, Mr. Secret Agent Man, are blabbing about quaint Victorian houses and cud-chewing cows? It's *my* life that's supposed to be in danger here. You owe me a decent explanation."

He sighed. "Whatever you do, *don't* turn around."

She turned around.

"Hey! I told you not to do that."

She gave him a sheepish look. "Sorry. It's kind of instinctive, you know? You tell someone not to look, and of course, they look. What don't you want me to look at?"

"Did you see the blue car behind us?"

"Sure. It's kind of frumpy with lots of dings and dangs and a whole bunch of miles under its belt."

"Well, that frumpy old Honda has been on our tail for about an hour now."

"Are you sure? This is a free road, you know. Anyone can travel a long way on it."

"That's nuts, Carlie. The car's been there, speeding when I speed, slowing when I slow. They even made the turn back when I last tried to make my route less direct."

She wrapped her fingers around the shoulder strap of her seat belt. Dan noted how white her knuckles turned.

"What do we do now?" she asked.

"Hang on tight," he said, his attention on the turn-off up ahead. At just the right moment, he spun onto the narrow side road.

Carlie gasped. "Whoa! I didn't sign up for this."

He snorted. "You signed up for trying to stay alive. If this is what it takes—oh, great. Look at that up ahead."

"Are those turkeys?"

Dan hit the brakes so as not to hit the back of the huge slow-moving truck. "Gobble, gobble, gobble."

With awe in her voice, Carlie said, "Wow! I've never

seen that many turkeys at once. Not even in the grocery store's freezer case at Thanksgiving."

"Forget the turkeys. The Honda just caught up with us."

She shot a glance over her shoulder. "So pass the turkeys."

"It's a narrow road, the truck's fat and I have a no-passing line. I can't see what's coming around the truck, Carlie. Do you want to take a chance on a head-on collision? So far, the blue Honda's not done a thing."

"Yeah, I'm willing to take my chances. Are you willing to give them the opportunity to pounce? If the guys behind us are who you think they are, then I'd rather try and dodge oncoming traffic. At least we have a chance there. Back here? We're sitting ducks…or turkeys, in our case."

He pulled to their left a bit, but couldn't see much. He got back in line behind the noisy birds. She had a point. If he swerved and no car hit them, then they had a chance to speed up and put some distance between them and the Honda. If he stayed where he was, then he'd lead the Honda right to where they were going.

"Okay." He took a deep breath. "Here goes nothing."

"Go for it. The Lord is with me, and if it's my time, then it's my time."

"Well, it's *not* mine." He held his breath and pulled into the opposite lane. He accelerated, and as he did, caught sight of what was in front of the turkey truck.

Another turkey truck.

"Why does this have to happen to me?" he muttered under his breath. What should he do? Stay in the wrong lane and try to pass the fowl or slow down back to where he'd been?

"Oh, no!" Carlie cried, her voice shrill. "Two trucks."

And then it came to him. "Watch this."

With a quick twist of the steering wheel, he slid in between the rolling loads of Thanksgiving dinners. The truck he'd followed, now behind him, honked its loud, bass horn. Dan rolled down his window, waved what he hoped the trucker would take as an apology, but never took his eyes off the feathered friends up ahead.

"Can you explain this to me?" Carlie asked. "We're trapped here. I don't get it."

"You know how your family's friends hate witnesses?" He jabbed a thumb over his shoulder. "There's a witness. I doubt they're going to pop us with that guy watching."

"What if they pull up beside us, shoot us, then speed away. The truck smushes us into the other one, the witness is good for nothing, and Tony's pals get what they wanted all along."

He shrugged. "It could happen that way, but I don't think it will. If they were going to pull that kind of stunt, they'd have done it already. They don't want to give the trucker more time to notice them than necessary."

He hoped.

The gamble had been risky, but he was in an all-or-nothing situation…or so he thought. There was always the slim chance the blue Honda belonged to some flaky driver who got a thrill out of following people down back roads.

He didn't think that was the case.

"How far do you think these turkeys are going?" Carlie asked after a dozen miles of silence.

"Beats me, but I hope it's somewhere down in Florida."

"If that's your plan, then we're in big trouble."

"Glad you finally figured it out. We've been in big trouble from the start."

She gnawed on her bottom lip, then drooped against the car window, closed her eyes, laced her fingers on her lap, and didn't say another word.

That's when the ticklish thought that had danced in his mind grew and grew. In seconds, it crowded out every other thought. How had they been found? He'd called the office from the hospital, but he hadn't spoken with anyone after that. And he'd taken Carlie's cell phone away a long time ago.

As far as he knew, the only people who knew their destination were Carlie, Eliza and himself. Had they been followed to the Millers' farm? If so, then why hadn't anything happened there? Had it been a matter of too many witnesses?

Or…

He really didn't want to consider the other options. For about a year now, he, J.Z. and David had suspected the presence of a mole at the Philly Bureau office. That possibility turned his stomach. Just the thought of someone who was supposed to be on the side of law, order and justice selling out to the mob set his blood to a boil.

But that was nothing compared to his other fear. Was Carlie really on the up-and-up? Or was she playing some kind of sick mob game?

True, she'd helped Maryanne, but she could have

done that out of simple friendship. The two women had gotten pretty tight in a very short time.

And her father and brother were sitting behind bars. Blood is thicker than water and all that.

Had she changed her mind? Had she decided to turn again? Was she helping the mob? Was she leaking info to them? Had she had a chance to use a phone at the hospital?

He shot her another look. Again, that aura of peace had descended on her as she slept. Just looking at Carlie Verdi Papparelli made him smile. In spite of his training, his suspicions and common sense. He remembered when he'd given J.Z. a hard time when his partner had been in a similar position.

Difference was, Maryanne Wellborn, now Prophet— J.Z.'s wife—had clearly been the victim of mistaken identity. In his case, there was no chance of a mistake. Carlie was a member of the Verdi family. She had married into the Papparelli family. She had all those ties J.Z. had believed Maryanne had. In the end, J.Z.'s suspicions had been wrong. Would Dan's prove to be as well?

Only time would tell.

Dan turned his attention back to the driving and focused on the truck full of turkeys again.

But he couldn't keep thoughts from popping up. And one particular one stuck with dogged stubbornness. Were he and Carlie headed for slaughter just like the fowl ahead? He hoped not.

All he knew was that he couldn't count on anything but his own powers. Well, he could trust David Latham. And J. Z. Prophet. He didn't know when or how, but the moment he thought it safe enough to pull off the road and into a diner, gas station, truck stop…*whatever*…he would call J.Z.

Even though it made him nervous, Dan was going to have to reach out for help. He'd come to a point where his training, his strength, his experience might not be enough.

He had to put his faith somewhere. And his partner was all he had. He hoped it was enough.

Carlie's life depended on it.

SIX

Something changed after they swooped in between the two turkey trucks. Carlie had no idea what might have caused the change, but she did know that Dan's expression had turned grim, and he hadn't said anything else.

He'd also changed tactics after the incident. Up until then, Dan had kept to back roads. But once the turkey trucks turned onto a main highway, he made a comment about the Honda no longer following, and he'd sped ahead of the gobblers. He'd resumed his strong-and-silent mode after that, and now, a couple of hungry hours later, civilization approached.

She couldn't stand the silence anymore. "What happened with the Robert Frost plan? You know, staying on the road 'less traveled by'?"

"Changed my mind."

She blew her wispy bangs off her forehead in exasperation. "I know that. I want to know why."

"Simple. They caught up to us on the back roads, so I decided to mingle."

"Is that a good idea?"

"Beats me. Right now, all I want is food and a men's room, not necessarily in that order."

"Excellent! My bladder's in agreement with yours."

He muttered something about small favors.

Carlie bit her bottom lip. Had she done something that made him mad, something to make him act like this? She wasn't sure what the *this* really was; she just didn't like the silent treatment.

"Okay, Danny Boy," she said when she couldn't stand the situation a moment longer. "Care to tell me what I did wrong this time?"

Unless she was much mistaken, he winced. "Ah…I don't *think* you did anything, did you?"

The look he shot her seemed filled with unspoken meaning, but she, of course, couldn't read minds or weird looks. "You're going to have to do better than that."

"How 'bout you let me do my job?"

"How 'bout you cut the witness a break?"

"Tell you what. We're going to go find a place to eat. How's that for keeping you informed?"

"Lousy. Tell me where you're taking me."

"Hmm…I'm not sure yet. I'm going to have to count on a lightning bolt of inspiration. But I'm hoping for a busy place, one where we can blend in with the crowd."

"Boy, you really made a turnaround."

"It's called being flexible."

"Pretzel-like, aren't you— Hey! Look at that. We're almost in Charleston. How cool!"

"I aim to please, ma'am."

"If only you'd said that without the sarcasm…" She

leaned forward, looked from side to side, as though to capture every sight. "I've always wanted to visit Charleston. Everything I've read about the city says its historic district is wonderful."

He let out a gust of breath. "I don't remember anything about sightseeing."

"And here I thought all that pointing at cows and barns signaled a change in your approach."

"*Now* who's being sarcastic?"

"I'm just going crazy, Dan. Think about it. How'd you like to be in my shoes?"

His grin surprised her with its full dose of mischief. "No way! You couldn't pay me enough to wear those neck-breaker heels of yours."

She lifted her left foot. "These? They're no big deal, they're just shoes."

"Big being the operative word, right?"

She shrugged. "So…are you going to hit the fast food again, or do we vary our diet today?"

"Since you ask so nicely, we'll vary the diet. But first I have to find my way into the city, find parking, get oriented…you get the picture."

"In other words, 'shut up, Carlie,' right?"

"I didn't say that."

"No, but you thought it." She grinned. "Tell you what. I'll forgive you if you take me to the historical district. At the very least, let me see Broad Street. I've read they've preserved the area, and it's great for shopping and business."

"Let's see here. You're on the run from the mob, but you want to go shopping?"

"I'd love to go shopping, but you took away my credit cards a long time ago. I have no way to access funds until we get to Florida. You said the Bureau would transfer my money and I could access it there. Until then, I'm broke."

He looked sheepish, but only for a moment. "You know the paper trail of credit cards is very easy to trace, don't you?"

She dragged out her last ounce of patience. "If you tell me that one more time, Dan, I'll scream."

"Don't do that. Just sit back, and enjoy the ride into town."

A ride that seemed destined for brevity. "Look!" he said minutes later. "Breakfast."

Carlie glanced in the direction he indicated, and nearly cried. "We're in a city known for history, shopping, and amazing eats, and you want to feed me at IHOP?"

"What's wrong with pancakes?" he asked as he turned into the chain restaurant's parking lot. "And they have awesome syrup."

"Sure, I love them, too, but we're by the ocean." She tried her best puppy-dog look. "Besides, breakfast was hours ago. C'mon, Danny Boy. Let's find us some seafood. Pleeeeeze…"

She didn't need a PhD in rocket science to figure out he'd soon need a dentist. The frequency with which Dan ground his teeth couldn't possibly be good for them.

When his jaw muscles stopped working under his taut skin, he said, "Fine. We'll go find seafood. It may take us a while, though. Remember, I'm not familiar with the city."

"Thanks! And I don't mind a little longer wait. Not while you drive through a town I've always wanted to visit."

"Just keep it down. I need to concentrate. Don't distract me."

This call for silence had more oomph behind it than others that came before. Carlie knew no more now than twenty minutes earlier, and yet nothing remotely beautiful appeared on the horizon. So, since she was helpless, she turned to the One Who held everything in His hands. She prayed.

Carlie's excitement returned as they drove into the heart of the old city. Beautiful buildings from another era lined the streets. The town's charm transported her back in time.

Then she spotted a street sign. "Oh, look, look, look! We're on King Street."

"Another famous street you want to scope out?"

"Oh, yeah! *The* best antique shops, dress shops, and some faboo places to eat, too."

"How about some excellent parking?"

"Hmm…" She looked to the right, the left, and found nothing. "That's your job. You're behind the wheel. It'll be the perfect division of labor. You find the parking, and I'll choose the food."

His lips quirked up in another grin. Wow! Two in less than an hour. How'd she suddenly rate?

"You got me there," he said. "Go for it. I'll spring for a lunch of your choice."

"As if *you* had a choice—you have to feed me. I have no money, remember?"

He didn't bother to respond. Not more than five minutes later, he'd found a spot on a side street. They got out of the car, he put a handful of coins in the parking meter, and they headed back toward King Street.

"You are such a spoilsport," she declared a little later. "You bring me here, where the shopping's world-class, and you won't let me go into even one store. What's up with that?"

"Earth to Carlie! We're not real tourists here, remember? You wanted to see King Street, and you're seeing King Street. We've determined that you don't have any dough, so it makes no sense to waste time bopping in and out of stores. No money, no shopping. Besides, I'm hungry."

Carlie wrinkled her nose. "Okay, you win that one. But only because I'm hungry, too. There!" She pointed up ahead. "That's where I want to eat."

"'FISH'? In all upper-case letters?"

"You agreed on seafood. It can't get much clearer than that. Besides, I read a killer review in *American Foodie* magazine. They raved about the food."

"Lead the way."

The restaurant lived up to its praise. Carlie ordered shrimp and grits, a local delicacy recommended by the reviewer. And the dish didn't disappoint. The grits, contrary to what she'd expected from tales of northern visitors to the South, had no lumps, and the shrimp were fresh and tender.

"Yum!" she said, leaning back when she'd finished her meal. "You have to agree. This is way better than IHOP."

Dan shrugged. "Each has its own charm."

"Okay, you have a point. But I see nothing left of that massive lobster you ordered. There's no lobster at IHOP."

"And there's no boysenberry syrup here at FISH."

"Touché!"

They ordered dessert, and relished every bit of that, too. Then Dan dropped his napkin on the table. "Let's go. Time to split."

"You're not going to lock me up in that car again already, are you?"

"I don't know a better way to get you down to Florida and that place the Bureau's arranged for you."

"Aw…be a sport. A couple of hours won't make that much difference."

He rolled his eyes. "But at the first sign of trouble, it's my way, okay?"

"Sure, your way *and* the highway—I get it. You're still the boss."

They walked down King Street, and soon Carlie had another idea. "Since we're here, would you indulge me one last little bit?"

"Now what?"

"Aren't you the cheerleader, oozing with enthusiasm! All I want is to go down to the Battery. It's so famous, and the views of the ocean are supposed to be fantastic. So…how about it?"

Carlie watched him wrestle. And she supposed it wasn't the brightest idea, since they were trying to flee from killers, but she needed a break. The tension of the past few months was about to drive her nuts.

"Let's go—"

"Oh, Dan, thanks—"

"Don't thank me yet. Wait until you're done testifying. That's when I'll be done with my job, and you'll have your life back."

"Hey, little things mean a lot."

And then, as they headed for the waterfront walkway and park, Carlie fell in love with the gorgeous, pastel-painted mansions that lined the street on the way to the Battery area. "They're beautiful! Don't they look like giant wedding cakes?"

"Huh?"

She blew her bangs off her forehead. "Spoken like a true male. It's those white, white balconies across each floor of the mansions, Dan. They contrast so well against the pink and yellow and blue of the walls. And the turned spindle balusters…they look like thick, intricate ribbons of icing…."

He took hold of her elbow at the street corner and led her to the waterfront park. As they crossed, a horse-drawn tour-bus rolled up to the T-type intersection.

"Isn't this wonderful?" Carlie cried. "Can't we just stay here? Can't the Bureau find me a place in Charleston?"

Dan shrugged. "I supposed they could, but they didn't. Everything's set in Orlando. The most important things, security and protection, are in place there."

Carlie sighed. "I suppose."

The disappointment stung, but she refused to let it get her down. After all, she was in the fabulous city of Charleston. She didn't know when she'd get another chance to come back.

In the park, the gazebo drew her. She hurried over, then spread her arms wide and spun around. "Can't you just see what it must have been like all those years ago?"

"Sorry," Dan muttered. "I'm too busy watching out for your 'family.'"

"No, really. Take a look at the gazebo…the water just beyond. Imagine me and a group of my girlfriends in our hoop skirts, fans and parasols…."

"I'm more concerned with reality."

"Well, this place looks pretty real to me— Ouch!"

Carlie never saw what hit her. She just knew that it hit her in the back, and hard. She stumbled, fell. When she caught her breath, she looked around, but before she could focus on any one thing, Dan yelled, "Go! Run!"

Carlie crawled up onto her knees, and then stood. "Where?" She looked around. "Where do you want me to go?"

"Just *go!* I'll catch up to you."

With a final glance at the water, the gazebo, the stunningly beautiful homes, Carlie saw no one who looked dangerous or even familiar, but she didn't dare take any more risks, at least not right then. She wasn't sure where to go, but she started to run.

Running wasn't easy, certainly not in her Manolos. Her ankles bobbled, but her fierce determination served her well. Then heavy footsteps pounded up behind her. Someone ran up to her side, grabbed her hand, and dragged her sideways.

"It's me," Dan said. "I'm not sure where we're headed. But we do have to leave." He breathed in rough drags of air. "Not just the Battery, but Charleston."

Another twisted footstep wrenched Carlie's ankle, but she refused to be beaten. She kept going. "I know. And I'm sorry."

Then she heard more footsteps behind them. "Hey, mister! Lady! What'd you do with our mini-Frisbee? We're real sorry we hit you, Robbie's just got lousy aim."

The child's voice was the least dangerous sound Carlie had ever heard. She glanced at Dan. He turned his head. She did the same. He stopped.

She didn't. Until her right heel sank into…something. She heard a POP! and then went down.

"Aw, great," she groaned. "Now what am I going to do?"

Dan looked her way then back at the three boys and a woman, more than likely their mother. Finally, he turned to Carlie again. "Just ditch them. I never could figure out why you insisted on wearing the stupid things."

"You want me to go barefoot?"

"What do you want to do, limp your way to Florida?"

"I need shoes! Most restaurants are 'no shoes, no shirt, no service,' and I'm going to want food again before we're anywhere near Orlando."

Dan rolled his eyes, then turned back to the kids. "Your Frisbee's back where it landed. Sorry for the confusion, and my friend's fine. Don't worry about her."

"Easy for you to say," she muttered as she removed her unbroken shoe. She walked over to a trashcan nearby. "But I'll forgive you after you've replaced my footwear."

"I guess you'll get your way, after all."

"Really?" A zip of excitement ran through her. "King Street?"

"Lead the way, Cinderella. Looks like you're in the market for a slipper, magic or otherwise."

And so they shopped.

For shoes.

But the shoes were nothing like what she'd ever owned.

"Love them or leave them," Dan said, arms crossed, jaw like granite.

Carlie sighed. "I won't love 'em, but I'm not about to leave 'em, you style-less boor."

And so, with no further flourish, she donned the thick-soled pink-rubber thong sandals he'd found at a drugstore around the corner from King Street. So much for her shopping trip.

Orlando, here she came.

"Here," Dan said, relieved. "This is it!"

Disbelief opened her eyes wide. "No way!"

"No joke." Now that the idea had enough time to work its way through his mind, with every passing second, Dan grew more certain. "Sometimes the best hiding place is right out in the open. And you can't get much more open than public transportation."

"But a bus?"

"Hey, it's going south. So are we. It's a perfect fit."

"What about the car? My clothes? They're in the trunk."

"They're not worth your life. We'll get you new clothes."

She glanced at her sandals. "If these are any indication of what you'll spring for, then I'm in trouble—or in disguise, whichever you prefer."

He bought the tickets, and ignored Carlie's litany of questions and opinions, none of which struck him as positive. Still, he didn't dare retrieve the car. Although the event at the park had been more of a non-event, he'd landed back on earth with a heavy *thud* of reality. He never should've let Carlie talk him into the sightseeing excursion.

"From here on in, it's caution to the max," he added. "I intend to get you to that witness stand in one piece, no matter what."

They boarded the bus at the very last possible minute. He hadn't wanted to buy the tickets too far in advance of departure. That would have made it easy for anyone following them to figure out their destination. This leg of their trip would get them to Sarasota. There, he'd buy another pair of tickets, and they'd head for St. Petersburg. Finally, at the beachfront city he'd buy them seats to Orlando, and hopefully they'd arrive at their destination without further incident.

Why did he always get stuck with the weird ones? Cases, that is. Carlie? Well, she was different, but he wouldn't classify her as particularly weird.

Especially not when, not more than fifteen minutes into their bus trip, she fell asleep. Yes, she again wore that peaceful look, but that wasn't what reached deep inside him. She disarmed him, quite innocently, when her head drooped.

Onto him.

His shoulder seemed to fit the bill for a pillow. With

a soft sigh, Carlie nestled closer to him. Her gesture filled Dan with a warmth that surprised him. And gentleness.

A rush of protectiveness left him breathless.

He couldn't tear his gaze away from his charge. A smile broke loose even though he knew all the dangers Carlie posed. There was just something about the mobster's widow.

"Oh, my. That is so precious."

Dan jolted his attention back to the present situation. A woman with spiky, eggplant colored hair sat across the aisle from him, a super-pleased look on her face.

"Huh?" Oh, yes. He could be so, so eloquent at the most inappropriate times.

She gave him a little wave. "Yes, dear. It's lovely to see you still in the first blush. I can always pick out the fresh ones. These are the memories you treasure years later."

"I'm sorry, ma'am, but I don't understand."

"I just love young love. I'm an expert, you know."

"Ah…an expert?"

She preened—and now Dan knew exactly what that meant. With a knowing smile on her fuchsia-pink lips, the middle-aged woman patted the quilted, floral-fabric bag on her lap, which made a paper-crinkling sound. "I'm Antonesia Sweetinghouse."

The name meant nothing to Dan. "Pleased to meet you."

She gasped. "You don't recognize me? I'm the author of *Love, Love Me Forever*. It's a historical romance. And Hollywood's just bought the rights. It's going to be a movie."

What did a guy say to that? "I…see."

"Uh-huh." She leaned across the aisle. "I'll bet you they get Nicole Kidman to play Esmerelda Lucille."

Just then, before he was forced to respond, the bus driver applied the brakes, and Antonesia stood. "Take it from me, dear. Your bride's a lucky girl. I hope you don't hide your gentle tenderness from her. A woman needs to know herself loved and treasured, and you're doing it just the right way. Congratulations. I wish you two darling newlyweds many years of happiness. Oh, and a couple of kids, too."

She left him stunned.

Speechless.

Jaw agape.

Of course, they weren't newlyweds. They weren't even married.

In fact, the poor lady would surely be horrified to learn that Carlie had actually been married to the mob.

Thank goodness his companion hadn't heard that conversation. Protecting Carlie was hard enough. He didn't need a witness with thoughts of romance in her head.

SEVEN

They reached Atlanta late that night. Dan was tired and, to be honest, cranky. This crazy venture—he couldn't call it an assignment, it was so offbeat—hadn't followed any normal, familiar pattern so far. And Carlie wasn't the kind of person Dan usually dealt with.

Turkeys…Frisbees…*escape buses?*

Not the stuff of typical FBI assignments, that's for sure.

"Don't even think of leaving this room," he warned Carlie. "I don't think we've been followed this time, but I can't be sure."

She shrugged. "They have guns, remember? There's not a whole lot I can do if they show up and blow the lock off the door."

"But you can minimize the chances they'll find you. Don't show yourself, and they won't know you're here. That's how you control the chances of being spotted."

She sagged against the plain beige door. "Look, Dan, I'm so tired that when I hit that bed, I won't even stick my nose out from under the covers. I doubt I'll wake up until you decide to pound on my door in the morning."

"I won't pound. How about I call you? On the room phone."

A weak grin made an effort to brighten her face. "My own private wake-up-call service."

"We aim to please, ma'am."

"Good night, Dan."

He waited until he heard her slip the chain lock into place. Then, just as exhausted as Carlie, he took the ten steps to the door of the room next to hers. If anything was to come down, then he wanted to be as close as possible so he could act.

The cheap chain-motel's room offered few amenities, but at least it was clean. He headed straight for the bathroom, showered, and then rummaged through the Wal-Mart bag that held his few possessions.

Shopping at the discount giant with Carlie had been an experience. He'd expected her to turn up her nose at the decent but inexpensive garments, but instead she'd enjoyed her spree. And he'd floundered when she'd insisted on a visit to the beauty aisles. What did he know about skin and hair care and makeup?

He'd had to curb her enthusiasm; they could only carry so much and still be as nimble as he needed them to be. Now, he suspected she'd make the sturdy jeans and simple tops she chose look like more than they really were.

After he'd let the hot-as-he-could-stand water pummel his tense shoulders long enough, he crawled into bed, set the bedside alarm clock for seven, and clicked off the lamp. He welcomed the soothing embrace of the night's darkness.

Brrriiiiing!

The light on his cell phone display window guided him to the irritating if necessary gadget. "Hullo?

"How's it going?" David Latham asked.

Dan gave a humorless chuckle. "Trust me. You don't want to know."

"*That* good?"

"Worse."

"So where are you right now?"

"In a cheap motel in downtown Atlanta."

"How'd you wind up there?"

Dan reached up and flicked the lamp back on. "Trying to avoid Carlie's relatives.'"

Silence. Then, "But I thought you were headed for a safe house. Didn't you say that was somewhere in Orlando?"

"That's the plan. We're just taking—" he remembered Carlie's enjoyment of the sights and sounds along the way "—the scenic route."

"Oh-kay. I have to assume something happened between here and there."

"Gobble, gobble."

"Huh?"

Dan recounted the fowl escapade. He winced at David's hearty laughter. "You wouldn't find it so funny if you'd been the one behind the wheel."

"True, I probably would've been stressed—"

"Try near panicked, bro. There's no question that blue car was on our tail. Remember J.Z. and his bullet-dodging drive down a country road? I expected shot-out windows at any second."

"Hmm…. Wonder why they didn't shoot? The mob's not known for its benevolence."

Dan snorted. "Yeah, benevolence. Right." He hadn't thought about the lack of bullets. "At the time, I didn't stop to think, but now that you mention it, it is strange. They stayed behind us for miles with no other cars on the road."

"I wonder if that might have something to do with Carlie being Verdi's little girl."

"Do you really think her father's trying to kill her? He might be furious with her. I'm sure he sees her turning state's evidence as a betrayal, but I don't think he'd kill her—have her killed."

"I agree. I don't think it's Verdi after her. But I do know he still has clout with many on the outside. They'd want to be very careful around his daughter. Even with Verdi himself behind bars."

"Are you trying to tell me you think we're dealing with 'conflicted' mobsters? The kind who, even though they don't want her to testify, are scared to kill her?" He tugged on a loose thread from the floral bedspread. "Doesn't sound like any mobsters I know."

David didn't answer right away. "I'm with you. This isn't typical of organized crime. Usually, they just shoot and run. But if you'll remember, things were pretty weird on the DiStefano case, too."

"Sure. Mummers and their sequined costumes are not the first things that come to mind when you think of mobsters."

"How about the investigation into Papparelli's dirty

dealings in nursing homes? Don't forget that weird deal with your merry widow's late husband's empty casket and its trip to Sicily."

It was Dan's turn to pause and think. "You may have something there. We've been looking at this as separate assignments, related only by the mob's usual tentacles and Carlie's husband's actions. But what if…what if there's more to these cases? What if they're all part of a larger picture?"

"How so?"

"I hate to even go there, but J.Z. insisted there was a mole in the office, and then you had that DiStefano file lifted." Dan took a deep breath. "Now a tail catches up to us in the most unexpected place. I went out of my way to meander around. No direct paths from point A to point B. We were on an otherwise deserted backcountry road. I doubt they sort of stumbled upon us by coincidence."

"They must have planted a tracking device on you."

Dan bristled. "Not on me, man. But you might have something there. We were still driving the car I'd used in New Jersey."

"And you ditched it in Charleston. Did you call in the location to the office?"

"Not yet. I haven't had much time to do anything but run."

David's voice turned thoughtful. "What if…?"

"What if I call, and we watch to see what happens next?"

David's relief came across loud and clear. "I didn't know how you'd take my suggestion. You're always such a self-sufficient, stubborn mule that on a regular case J.Z. has to fight to remind you what it means to have a partner. This case may take more than what you can do on your own."

"Hey, I'm not that bad. And a good idea is a good idea. I think it's a good idea to test that mole theory once and for all. True, any call I make can be traced, but I can pop in to a library and e-mail Eliza."

"Well, that can be traced too—"

"Sure. But it takes longer, and Zelda of the magic computer fingers retired. Whoever's taken her place can't possibly be as good as she is."

"Hah! You need to spend more time in the office, pal. Cindy Newton's a true computer nerd—and I'm not insulting her. That's how she describes herself. She also happens to have a master's in computer forensics. There's nothing she can't do to or with a computer hard drive."

"It'll still be slower than tracing a cell phone or even a landline."

"Not if you use a public phone. I know that in this day of cell phones, pay phones have become almost obsolete, but they're still out there. Tracing a call from one of them still takes a warrant. That's what takes time."

"Okay. I'll do the pay phone gig. We'll see if someone takes the bait."

"You mean, do they go for the car, or do they follow you? Am I right?"

"That's the plan."

"I'll try to sniff out who has turned—if anyone. And I'll check in with you on a regular basis."

"Great. Keep J.Z. up-to-date, will ya?"

"No problem. In fact, I'll have him keep his eyes and ears open at the office. Our two sets should be better than just my own." Then David paused again. "How does this assignment look time-wise? D'you think you'll be able to make my wedding? Lauren's decided on a Thanksgiving week date."

"Aw, man. We're looking at Labor Day round the corner here. Verdi's trial won't come up anywhere near as soon as a couple of months."

"Any chance you could get someone to do back-up so you can come?"

"And leave Carlie behind?" Dan chuckled. "I doubt the woman would miss a wedding, any wedding, just because she's supposed to be in hiding."

David laughed. "Yeah. I'd have to say Carlie has a mind of her own. And she'd certainly want to see J.Z.'s wife again. They became good friends, and she'll know Maryanne will be at our wedding. Well, I'll be disappointed if you can't make it."

"So will I."

"But we'll keep on praying for you and Carlie."

Dan didn't know what to say—as usual. "Uh, well, yeah. Sure. Now, I'd better get some sleep. I need to be on my toes to keep up with Carlie."

"Not the bad guys, huh?"

"Not them. I want to hurry and stay a whole lot of steps ahead of them."

They said their goodbyes, and Dan hung up. Why was everyone he knew so religious? It made him uncomfortable. He couldn't understand their faith. He could only put his faith in himself and his training.

And then he turned off his light. The darkness descended again, but this time, it wasn't nearly as comforting as it had been before. Now, the depth of the night went on like an unending void. He'd experienced the same sensation before, had tried to ignore the emptiness that came with it.

Carlie's words came back. "Loneliness…"

He couldn't believe there was a God out there in the ether. All he knew was this deep lack of light, where he was on his own, with no one to turn to.

And he was fine with that.

Yes. Of course he was. That's the way it had always been. And how it always would be.

With his usual determination, Dan rolled over and willed himself asleep.

The next morning Carlie woke up without any help from the alarm clock, or even from her very own secret agent man. She stretched, stood, grabbed her little bag of Wal-Mart goodies, and headed for the shower.

A short while later, in a pair of comfortable jeans and a fluttery gauze top she'd bought at Wal-Mart, she brushed out her wet, tangled hair, and sat to watch cable news on the motel room's TV. It would've been great if by some weird coincidence the anchor had relayed information about her father's and brother's cases. But this was real life and not fiction. All she got from the program was more on the war on terror, the price of a barrel of oil, the health of the stock exchange and inflation.

Right around the time her stomach's growling began

to drown out the news, Dan called her from outside her door—no phone call, as he'd promised. Instead, he knocked. "You awake yet, Rip van Winkle?"

She opened the door, and smiled. "Watch it, buddy. I'm not some old man who forgot to wake up."

A strange expression crossed his face. "Trust me, Carlie. There's no way to mistake you for anyone of a certain vintage."

She couldn't be sure, but Carlie thought he'd paid her a weird kind of compliment…reluctantly. His penetrating gaze got to her, and she blushed.

To keep him from seeing her discomfort, she headed back to the bathroom for her bag of goodies. "I'm ready to head out whenever you are," she said on her way back.

He nodded, turned, then paused. "Uhm…I'd better warn you. I don't have a firm plan in hand. I'm going to have to play it by ear."

Carlie laughed. "And that's different from the past few days because…?"

Over his left shoulder, he shot her a crooked grin. "You got me there. Let me rephrase that. We're going to keep on playing it by ear."

This morning he put them back on their old dietary plan. Fast food was her only choice. Then, after they dumped the breakfast debris, he led her outside. He set off on foot at a brisk pace, his expression focused and purposeful. If anyone bothered to pay them any attention, the observer would probably think they had places to go, people to see.

Which Carlie figured was Dan's goal.

After they'd trudged around for about an hour, he stunned her by swerving to a curbside pay phone. The thing looked ratty and had long ago seen better days, but as rare as public phones had become in the current cell phone culture, that they even found one was a plus.

He further stunned her when he began to talk to his boss. She'd expected him to check in with the woman every so often, but she hadn't given the abandoned car much thought. Dan made a point of telling Eliza Roberts precisely where he'd left the bland beige sedan.

Then he fell silent. As the moments sped by and he didn't say another word, Carlie's curiosity got the better of her. By the time she turned around and took a good look at him, his face had turned lobster red, and she thought that, had they been characters in a cartoon, smoke would have started to spew from his ears.

But since this was real, no smoke escaped. His anger, however, became more obvious and ominous with every passing second. Uncomfortable, Carlie turned away, and took the time to check out their surroundings.

And she laughed.

Across the street and down a bit, she spotted a sign that read Fish Market. As if the sign wasn't enough, out the top of the roof of the building, a giant fish statue rose like abnormal antennae. Carlie had never seen a weirder statue. She doubted one would find a larger statue of a fish anywhere else in the world.

As she stared, she became aware of a presence at her side. Her heart kicked up its beat, and for a split second, she feared for her life. But she held her ground and spared a glance. To her relief, it was her intense secret agent man, more intense than ever.

"What's up?" she asked.

She watched Dan's remarkable display of self-control and determination. He deliberately lost the hard lines of the expression he'd worn since he dialed his boss's number, and his shoulders eased down.

He nodded toward the market. "Looks like someone's idea of a fish out of water is what's up around here." He then made a shark shape with his hands, his thumbs mimicking the fin. "*Tum, tum, tum, tum...*"

She chuckled at his reproduction of *Jaws*. "Interesting way to put it."

"Interesting way to top a building."

"Can't say anyone would ever mistake the place for anything other than what it is."

He crossed his arms and smiled—a tight smile, but still a smile. "So you think this is more obvious than the name of the restaurant in Charleston?"

"Just slightly."

Carlie noticed a hint of his earlier strain had returned to his voice, even though she suspected he thought he'd hidden it well behind that smile. "Care to tell me what's wrong?"

His eyes narrowed. "Eliza's not my favorite person."

"That's it? You don't like your boss?" She didn't buy it. But it soon became obvious he wouldn't try to sell her anything else. Fine.

"Okay, then," she said. "You're not talking, and we're just standing here like a pair of targets. Care to fill me in on what part this plays in your plan? What comes next?"

He glanced again at the giant fish. "We head on down to Orlando."

"Care to elaborate on how we're going to do this?"

"Don't you remember? We're patronizing public transportation these days. Let's go find us a southern-bound bus."

Carlie groaned. "Okay, Secret Agent Man. Lead the way."

He tossed the giant fish a final look. "I just hope the teeth that come after us aren't as sharp as those up there."

Carlie didn't like the sound of what he'd said, but she didn't think she'd get anywhere if she tried to dig further. If she pushed, he'd likely retreat into his silent mode.

She didn't think she could stomach any more of the uneasiness she'd felt when he first dropped his harangue in exchange for the dense silence. She knew when to back down.

"Well, Dan. I'll expect some kind of an explanation once we get to know each other better. I'm sure that's what you're waiting for, right? Just a chance to get chummier. Of course, it doesn't make a difference to you that I'm trusting a total stranger with my life."

Then his expression changed. For the first time since she'd met him, he scared her.

His eyes narrowed. His cheeks drew taut. His stance resembled that of a cobra about to strike. "Let me tell you a secret, Carlie. You'd do best to keep up your guard. It may take you a while longer to figure it out, but I'll try and hurry along the lesson. Don't bother to place your trust in anyone—at least no one but yourself."

"I already told you, Dan. I trust God—"

"Fine. But you're setting yourself up for disaster. You can't count on anyone or anything but yourself." He drew a harsh breath, looked her over with an intensity he'd never displayed before. "Even the best of the best aren't trustworthy."

In the moment he paused to regain control of his temper, Carlie said, "I don't get it. What's wrong?"

"Oh, nothing. Just that it seems someone at the office has turned. I'm pretty sure we have a mole."

Carlie went cold. A shiver racked her, and she dropped her Wal-Mart shopping bag.

"The blue Honda," she whispered.

"Bingo!" he answered. "The blue Honda. Neither you nor I are dumb enough to think it was a coincidence, so that leaves us with only one other choice."

"Someone's been setting us up," she said, her head spinning. "My father has someone inside the FBI. No wonder he got away with so much for so long."

"Bright as well as beautiful," he countered.

Carlie would never consider that comment a compliment. The ferocity behind his words made her wonder if his warning hadn't been more pointed than she'd first thought it to be.

Was he warning her about himself?

Could she trust him?

Or did he think *she* was the one who'd ratted them out?

EIGHT

"Oh, it's adorable!" Carlie cooed.

Dan looked from Carlie to the small, dumpy, and squatty beige stucco house then back to Carlie again. "Are you looking at the same thing I am?"

She pointed to the unattractive structure. "That's so cute. Just look at the big window in the front, and the little shrub by the front door."

"You mean that dingy, cracked glass mess and the brown remains of what once must have been a shrub?"

She tipped up her chin. "You have to look beyond the superficial, Dan. Beauty isn't skin deep."

Hers just starts with her silky-smooth skin. The thought flashed through his mind before he had a chance to stop it. It shook him.

He couldn't afford to continue to take note of her beauty, external or otherwise. Especially since he'd begun to realize that she wasn't just a pretty face. There was something about Carlie's intense optimism that just floored him. And her friendliness was genuine. She seemed to like everyone she came across.

"Dan!"

Her voice revealed her impatience. She'd probably repeated his name more than a couple of times while he ruminated on her multiple qualities. The woman was more than dangerous; she was lethal to his peace of mind.

"Er…what?"

"Well, are you going to make me stand out here in this killer heat and just drool over my new home or are you going to let us in?"

Something didn't add up here. The woman had moved out of her father's mansion into her husband's showplace, and she now wanted Dan to believe she was ecstatic over a postage stamp–size derelict dump in a nondescript area of Orlando?

"No. Of course not." He fumbled in his pocket and withdrew his wallet. "Here's the key. Let's go into your palace, princess."

She glared. "I'll have you know I'm no princess."

He had to agree, but he wasn't about to tell her. "Yeah, yeah, yeah. Go tell it to the guy who sold you those shoes you used to wear. If those stilettos aren't princess slippers, then I don't know what is."

She waggled a pink-thong-sandaled foot at him. "A princess would never wear a pair of these. I've been wearing them, and guess what? The cushy sole's pretty comfortable."

He rolled his eyes. "I'll make you a regular person yet."

"Not unless you let this future regular person into that house, you won't. I'm sure this cute little Florida cottage has a bathroom somewhere inside."

What was a guy to say to a comment like that? He unlocked the front door, and the stuffy air slapped him across the face. "Oh, wow. This place has been closed for a while."

Carlie dashed right past him. "Fine, but when a girl's gotta go, a girl's gotta go."

"Wait! I haven't checked it out yet—"

The slam of what he assumed was the bathroom door cut him off. He couldn't believe she'd had him so off-kilter that she'd been able to barge inside ahead of him. For all they knew, a killer could be waiting for her in that bathroom she wanted so much to use.

But a few minutes later, her reappearance in the tiny living room told him the bathroom had been as empty as the rest of the house.

"Just so we get this straight," he said, leashing his anger. "You don't ever—never again, you got it?—go into any place that I haven't had the chance to search. Someone could've been waiting in that bathroom, his gun ready for you. You wouldn't've known what hit you."

She paled, drew a sharp breath. "I didn't even think about it—"

"That's the point, Carlie. You aren't trained to think that way. It comes second nature to me by now. Please let me do my job. Your life depends on it."

Her jerky nod told him how well he'd made his point. "I know Who really holds the length of my life in His hands, but I also know what your goal is. And I have to say, I do want my father, my brother, and all their buddies out of business. I know God wants me to help do that. I'll be more careful in the future."

A chastened Carlie, her bright and saucy smile gone, was as rare as dodo birds in Central Park. Maybe he'd finally made progress. He'd give her the benefit of the doubt…until she proved herself unworthy of that trust.

"Hey, it's really hot and humid in here," he said as a bead of sweat made its way from the base of his neck down the length of his spine. "I'm going to see if this place has an air conditioner."

"And if it doesn't?" she asked, her horror almost comical. "Do you think the Bureau would get me one? I don't know that I'll survive otherwise. I might just do an imitation of the Wicked Witch of the West. You know, 'I'm melting! Melting away!'"

Dan chuckled then turned toward the rear of the house. "Try and contain yourself, okay? Don't know what kind of help a puddle will be at trial—"

Knock, knock, knock!

He reached for his concealed weapon, spun and rushed back to the front door. He jerked his head toward the bedroom doors. "Go to the back room. I'll check this out."

He could see her struggle with his order, but then she squared her shoulders and did as he'd asked. He breathed only a bit easier.

"Who's there?" he called.

"Open up," a woman answered. "I'm safe. My name's Sonia Mendez. I'm with the U.S. Marshal Service. I'm to take over the custody of the witness."

The door to Carlie's "palace" creaked when he drew it open. "Can you prove it?"

The petite brunette nodded. "Of course. Here's my ID."

Of course, it looked legit. "Don't mind if I call in and make sure, okay?"

She grinned. "I'd probably report you if you didn't. I'd say you were falling down on the job if you just took my word or that of a card that can be easily falsified."

He suspected Sonia was clean, but he still followed through. Sure enough, she passed the test with flying colors. In fact, he learned she recently had been recognized for her work protecting an aging agent whose cover had been blown. Memories in the spy game stuck around for a long time. Sonia had kept the woman alive long enough to get her started on a new life abroad.

He clapped his phone shut. She was who she said she was, but he wasn't ready to turn Carlie's custody to a stranger.

Sonia winked. "Toldja."

"Da-an!" Carlie's voice held a hint of impatience. Impatience was one of her less appealing qualities—not that he was a fount of patience himself.

"Yes, Carlie. You can come out now."

She returned to the living room, and, not for the first time, her presence hit him with a punch. This woman was not one to be ignored. How could she have lived in the shadow of two criminals for so long? Sooner or later, he'd have to get her to open up. His curiosity about her was growing daily.

"Who're you?" she asked when she stood about five feet away from Sonia.

"I'm your friendly local U.S. Marshal." Sonia held

out a hand. Carlie shook it. The agent continued. "I'm the one who found the house, and I'm going to take over your protection while you're here in Orlando. I'll also provide liaison to the FBI."

Carlie glanced at Dan, a strange expression on her face. "D'you mean, I get to lose my shadow?"

Sonia laughed. "I don't think so. You just get to swap shadows."

"Won't it be too easy for someone to follow you, since you're local?"

"You'd be surprised how easy it is for me to slip under the radar here in Florida. And in Miami? Even my *mami* wouldn't be able to pick me out of a crowd of Latina women there."

Dan sent Sonia a grin. "I don't know about you. If this place is anything to go by, then I don't know that I want to trust what you'll call protection for Carlie."

Sonia clapped her fists on her slim hips. "What?" she asked, humor in her voice. "You don't like your accommodations? Picky, picky, picky."

Carlie reached out a hand, and placed it on Sonia's shoulder. "Pay no attention to him. He's the loudest shadow I've ever seen. And I like this place. It's going to be mine, at least for a while, and I can do pretty much what I want with it, right?"

Dan caught the speculative gleam in Sonia's black eyes. "You're making music for my ears," she said. "We wound up with the place after a drug bust, and what you just said fits your cover to perfection."

The little glance she sent his way made Dan uneasy. "What have you come up with?"

"Carlie's going to love it, since she likes the house and wants to work with it. You're supposed to be newlyweds who've just moved into their new home. Home improvement's the name of the game. But then you'll have to go away on business."

Dan groaned. Another "newlywed" scenario. It was getting to be too much. "Figures the Bureau would cash in on cheap labor to fix up a lousy investment."

Sonia chuckled. "The bad guys paid for the place with their dirty money, so there was no mortgage. The higher-ups figured it'd make a great place to stash Carlie. I happen to agree with them."

"Wait!" Carlie cried. "Just wait a minute. Do you mean I really, really get to fix this place however I want? I can paint the walls purple-striped-orange with yellow polka dots?"

Sonia wrinkled her nose. "If you must."

"Ooooh, yeah!" Carlie's cheer came with heartfelt emotion. "Well, I won't do anything gross. I couldn't stand to live that way, but I can't wait to fix a place for myself."

Dan thought back to the Papparelli mansion in Philly. He'd understood Carlie had decorated the whole beautiful place herself. This didn't make sense—there was a lot about this woman that didn't.

"I suppose I'm the brawn of the team here—at least temporarily," he said. "I'll haul and lug, drill, hammer and demolish—"

"Whoa!" Carlie grabbed his forearm. "There will be no demolition around here. I like the house as it is, and I'm calling the shots…at least in here."

The last she added in a more conciliatory voice.

"All right!"

Sonia's grin and cheer spelled trouble for him. "I can read between the lines," Dan said. "It's two of you against one of me. Even the end of this assignment isn't about to get any easier."

Carlie shrugged. "I don't know about easier or not. I just want to know if meals are going to take a more regular pattern from here on in."

Sonia gasped. "Do you mean to tell me he hasn't been feeding you well?"

Outrage exploded in Dan. "Hey! I've been feeding you—"

"Well, he has been feeding me, but it's been kind of hit or miss. And the menu?" She tsk-tsked. "How'd you like to go on a fast food diet?"

Sonia's dark eyes opened wide. "Uh-oh. Not my favorite."

Clearly encouraged, Carlie continued, to Dan's mounting discomfort and irritation.

"My feelings exactly," she said. "I'm about ready to do serious bodily harm to anyone who dares get between me and a piece of fresh fruit…a crunchy broccoli spear…a crisp, sweet carrot…"

Sonia laughed. "Then you're going to love what I have in my car."

Carlie's expression brightened. "Groceries?"

"Give me a hand," Sonia said on her way to the door. "You'll see."

Dan followed in the women's wake. Carlie had done it again. She'd made a friend in seconds. And this woman was supposed to be on his side. He'd lost control of his witness.

He just hoped he hadn't lost control of the case right before he was supposed to hand it over.

At the front door, Carlie called out, "Bye!"

Sonia tossed her a grin over her shoulder and waved.

Carlie turned to Dan. "I like her."

"You would," he grumbled. "She's like a miniature Latina version of you."

"Now that's a dumb thing to say. Just because we have a few things in common doesn't mean we're some kind of clones."

"Never said clones. Just that you're too much alike."

"It's not that bad. We like nice shoes, and now that she introduced me to it, I love Cuban food, too."

The succulent pork chops, black beans with rice, fried plantains, and garlicky yucca Sonia prepared were the stuff of culinary dreams.

Carlie didn't let him hit her with another nutty comment. "You're just afraid that there's two of us against the one of you. You just don't like to share, and you're going to have to be less of a control-freak from now on."

"We'll see about that. I'm still the agent in charge."

"But not for long," she said, not sure what she thought about Dan's imminent departure. Then she crossed to the threadbare sofa in the living room. "Isn't this sad?"

Dan shrugged. "I've seen worse. Don't forget. The government got this place in a drug bust. That kind of criminal doesn't really care much about the décor of the place where they make end-of-the-line transactions."

"I can't wait to start fixing it up." She took a good look at the cracked window. "How long do you think it'll take to get that replaced?"

"Beats me. It looks custom-made."

"I'll have to call around tomorrow morning. I think that's the first thing that has to go."

"And here I thought it would be the lousy furniture."

"True. It's pretty crummy, but the window's a matter of security. See? I'm not as bad as you like to think."

"Small comfort, you know."

"How 'bout this? I'm also going to call a locksmith. We need dead bolts on both the front and back doors."

"Getting warmer."

"Plus…since this is Florida, and since as we drove in to town I noticed some on a handful of houses, I'm also going to call to get some decorative iron bars on the windows."

"Oh, that'll really help. There's not a single home in this particular neighborhood with that kind of thing. If anyone's been following us, they'll pick up on the new additions in no time."

Alarm struck. "Do you really think we were followed?"

"I have no idea. But I can't drop my guard. Especially since I have my suspicions—"

"The mole." He nodded, and she went on. "Okay. Then I'll get on the furniture and paint and flooring—"

"Hey, *Trading Spaces* isn't your middle name, you know. You're here for a reason."

"Yes. I'm to resume some kind of life until my father

and brother go to trial. Since mob cases are notorious for taking practically forever to prosecute, then I have years to cool my heels. I intend to do it in this cozy little place—and with nice furniture."

His gaze intensified. She felt as though he could see clear through her. "Well, I can't say I blame you for wanting to make the house more comfortable."

"That's right. I don't care about how fancy I can make it. It's the comfort I care about. And if those comfy pieces happen to be nice-looking, then it's all good."

Those eyes of Dan's made her uncomfortable. She could tell he had something particular in mind, and she wasn't sure she wanted to know what it was.

But, as usual around this man, it didn't seem to matter what she preferred.

"Tell me something," he said, his voice gentle and persuasive. "I got a good look inside your home in Philly—at least, what was left after the bomb went off—and it was one of the most beautiful places I've ever seen. J.Z. told me you'd decorated it all yourself."

She shrugged. "Sure. I went to a bunch of furniture designers, ordered custom pieces with custom fabrics, ditto for wall coverings, and then hired an army of contractors to work their magic all over the place."

"And fixing up this dump excites you more than that did?"

"What can I say? That was a matter of phone calls and giving orders. Besides, everything had to have Carlo's approval, and believe me, he wasn't easy to please."

He leaned forward at her final words. She winced.

She'd said more than she'd meant to. "Well, I don't really mean—"

"What was it like, Carlie? Life with a mobster as a father and another one as a spouse isn't the norm. Tell me about it."

She drew back. "I'd have thought you knew everything there was to know about me."

"I know the facts, but I want to know about you. How did *you* feel?"

She stared at the faded plaid upholstery on the couch. "I didn't know anything else growing up. Daddy spoiled me silly, and I loved him like any normal little girl. Mom worked hard to keep things the way he wanted, but they always got along very well."

"You didn't see anything strange?"

"How's a child supposed to know strange from otherwise?"

"Okay, so as a child you were oblivious. What about your marriage? How'd you meet Carlo?"

Carlie didn't really want to go there, but she'd come to know Dan's persistence too well in the last few months. "I didn't ever actually meet Carlo. He was young at the time, but he was my father's associate even before I was born. He was always around."

"How did you know you loved him? Wanted to marry him? The age difference must have been a factor."

She squirmed. "I grew up understanding that everyone, my parents, their friends, and Carlo, expected me to marry him. I can't say it was a forced or arranged marriage, like they said in newspaper reports after he died, but I just knew what was expected. I never thought anything else."

"You didn't answer my first question. Did you love him?"

She rose, a knot in her stomach, walked away from him. "I was…fond of him. I always saw him as kind and caring. Don't forget, I married him right after I graduated high school. My school was girls only."

His eyebrows rose nearly to his hairline. "Wow! Not your normal courtship, then."

She turned and approached him. "Look, Dan. Nothing about my life has ever been normal, so don't try to see it that way. I didn't know a thing about my father's 'business,' and I sure didn't want to know anything about Carlo and his strange associates."

"You must have had some kind of suspicions, though."

"I just told you I didn't want to know anything about it…him…them. I'm guilty of turning a blind eye to bizarre circumstances, okay?"

He stood and placed his hands on her shoulders. "And that's why you were so determined to help Maryanne clear her name, save her father, save herself."

"Wouldn't you want to help someone whose life is threatened?"

"Why do you think I do the kind of work I do?"

She averted her gaze. "I suppose."

He sighed. "I suppose I understand a little more about you than I did ten minutes ago. That's something."

She stole a glance at him, and the tenderness on his

face stole her breath away. When she could draw air again, she said, "How so?"

"Guilt's a horrible burden, isn't it?"

"I'm not guilty. My father and brother are—"

"Yes, they're guilty by commission, but you feel guilty by omission. It's what you didn't do that weighs on you."

A knot in her throat kept her from answering. How had he known?

He curved a finger under her chin, made her meet his gaze. "Now you're trying to make up for those years when you didn't speak, aren't you?"

The tears began to flow down her cheeks. "Don't you understand? I might have prevented any number of murders if I'd spoken up!" A harsh sob tore through her throat. "How can I live with that? I know God's forgiven me, but I still bear responsibility for those deaths. I have to do whatever I can to keep Dad and Tony, their friends and enemies from killing again."

Then her irritating special agent man threw her for a loop. He wrapped his arms around her and pulled her close. He placed a hand on the back of her head, urged her to lean on him, offered his shoulder, then held her as she wept.

"Poor Carlie," he murmured. "Go ahead. Cry. I doubt you've ever let any of those feelings out...."

He went on, but she didn't hear anything else he said. She didn't have to. He'd been right from the start. She'd yet to cry a tear. She hadn't mourned her many losses. She hadn't even let the anger she carried bubble up.

It was way past time for her tears.

She just hadn't expected an FBI agent's warmth and

caring. She'd known about his strength. Put it all together, and he became a nearly irresistible package.

But she had to resist. For too many reasons.

For one, he'd spent his whole life on the right side of the law. For another, he was on his way out of her life.

Carlie cried.

NINE

The next day Carlie woke up with swollen eyes and a burden on her heart—the same burden she'd carried since the day she faced the reality she'd tried so hard to ignore. The only good thing that had come out of her crying jag was the realization that Dan Maddox was getting to her.

She had to watch herself around him.

Carlie had never been particularly attracted to anyone. Her relationship with Carlo had been almost that of a father and daughter. Now she faced this intense tawny lion daily, and she didn't know how to react. It would've been easier if Dan had been an irritating, overzealous, dry-as-dust FBI agent.

But his commitment to her safety, his genuine concern for her and his tenderness last night told her he was far more than she could handle. He even had a sense of humor.

She sort of wished things were different, that she was a different woman. Then, a simple attraction to an acceptable man would be something to explore. Instead, the widow of a slain mobster had no business indulging in an attraction to an FBI Special Agent, especially not the one charged with keeping her alive. She couldn't let that sort of wish become the real deal.

With a heavy dose of reluctance, she got out of bed and took a shower. Once done, she grabbed her wide-toothed comb and began to work loose the knots in her long hair. Then she grinned—a wry grin, but still a grin.

"I'm gonna wash that man right outta my hair...." she sang. She loved Rodgers and Hammerstein's *South Pacific* and just about every other one of those old musicals.

Done with the comb, she went to the living room, dripping hair spread over her shoulders. Who knew what it would look like without the use of a hairdryer? Neither Dan nor Sonia, with her short, curly style, had considered a dryer a necessity in life.

The living room boasted a small TV. Sonia had told her the Marshal's Service sprang for cable, since they expected Carlie to stay put most of the time. They knew even the most ingenious soul would go stark raving mad after any length of time in close to solitary confinement. She clicked on the television and surfed her way to an old-movie channel.

A quick trip to the kitchen provided her with breakfast. Granola bar and cup of pineapple-banana yogurt in hand, she dropped onto the lumpy couch and let the magic of old Hollywood whisk her troubled mind away to the land of make-believe.

But her enjoyment of the Bette Davis movie didn't

last long. About twenty minutes after she'd turned on the TV, Dan let himself into the house. His penetrating stare made her blush.

"How are you this morning?" he asked.

That question wanted more of an answer than whether she'd caught a sniffle or stubbed her toe. It made Carlie feel raw and emotionally naked. She hated the feeling. "Fine."

His gaze never left her face. "Funny what you consider fine. Your eyes—they're still puffy."

Carlie sent him a crooked grin. "What a gentleman to notice!"

This time he blushed. "Sorry. I was just worried about you. You went through a big upheaval last night."

"Do you really have to beat the dead horse to a pulp?"

"No, I just want to make sure you're okay." He sat next to her, picked up her empty yogurt cup, and waggled it at her. "I like strawberry-banana better."

She jerked a thumb over her shoulder. "There's one of those in the fridge. Sonia's an awesome shopper. Can't wait to hit the stores with her."

He sighed as he stood. "You might as well get ready for a long wait, then. I don't think it's wise for you to expose yourself at a mall or shopping center."

"You know? I kind of feel like Jeanie in that old TV show. You know, 'Yes, Master.'"

He put on a mock-angry expression. "I'm nowhere near as manic as Major Nelson."

"Are you a fan, too?"

"I've watched reruns. Is that what's on?" He glanced

at the TV. "Oh. Bette Davis. Isn't there anything better to watch?"

"What do you mean, better? There's a reason old movies like this are referred to as the Golden Age of Hollywood."

"Hmm…a fan of the dusty-musties."

She tipped up her chin. "A connoisseur of fine film-making. I love old movies. Especially the musicals."

"You and my mother. She goes nuts when Fred Astaire dances up walls and across ceilings."

"Love *An American in Paris*." Carlie winked, then sang, "'S wonderful…'s marvelous…"

"You really do sound like Mom, but you're at least thirty years younger. What's up with that?"

Great. So they were going for another session of let's-rake-up-Carlie's-crummy-past. Fine. He wanted to know? Well, she'd let him know.

"Remember all I told you last night? Well, it was kind of lonely at home growing up. I spent a lot of time in front of the TV. A little kid can really get caught up in the make-believe of old movies. Especially, like I already said, the musicals."

"Did you ever consider studying filmmaking? It's a very lucrative career—"

"I've had access to more money than I ever care to see again. It was ill-gotten, I don't know where to return it, yet it follows me. And I need it to live. That's what's in my bank account." She shuddered; now that she was on the other side, the memories weren't so good. "Besides, filmmaking's a tough field. Only a very few lucky ones make it. And can you see a mobster's daughter or wife getting into any kind of attention-getting career?"

"Yeah. I guess you do have a point there."

Then something bounced back into her mind; it took on a life all its own. She gave Dan as big a smile as she could conjure. "But my love of movies, Dan," she said, "is why I'm going to visit Universal City Studios while I'm here in Orlando."

He snorted. "Think again."

"Nah, nah, nah," she countered and wagged her finger just beyond his nose. "Not so fast, Mr. Secret Agent Man. You yourself gave me the reason why we're going to go do Universal."

His expression grew wary. "I don't think so. I'm all for keeping you out of sight and out of the line of fire. Universal doesn't strike me as a place I can even dream of securing."

Her smile widened. "That's just it, Dan. Remember what you said about the bus?"

"Aaaarrrgh!"

His exclamation of frustration struck her as funny, so she laughed.

"What do you find so funny?"

"That you're the one who did it to yourself." She gathered her hair into a loose ponytail high at the back of her head and then turned it into itself to make a self-sustaining knot of hair. "Ah…relief from the heat."

"No way! You're not going to change the subject. Hiding in plain view in a bus is one thing. Mingling with the crowds at an amusement park is another."

"Yep. It sure is. There's way more people I can blend in with at an amusement park. And you know I'm right."

His jaw muscles twitched. His lips thinned. His nostrils flared and his eyes narrowed. He was mad. Still, Carlie knew she'd won the round.

"There's no way you can even begin to blend in anywhere, Carlie Papparelli. No matter where you go you're a standout. But you made my earlier point well. And you may be stuck here for months longer than we can even imagine. Maybe even years."

"I sincerely pray morning and night that the Lord won't let it come to years. But hey, I'm going to get bored super-quick in here, so Universal's a great idea. Then we can do Disney."

Horror rushed into his face. "Don't hold your breath."

"Give it up, Danny Boy. You're going down—with Mickey, Minnie, Goofy and the seven dwarves. You can't stop the inevitable."

A dark cloud seemed to settle over him then. "That, Carlie, is exactly what I'm most afraid of. The mob rarely misses its target. I hope a hit on you doesn't turn out to be inevitable after all."

They continued to belabor the point until Carlie suddenly stood. "I need a nap. Talking with you is like riding a Ferris wheel. You don't go anywhere. You just sit there and spin circles."

Dan bit down on his frustration. "Just remember I'm in charge of your safety, and we won't argue again— no more Ferris wheel chats."

She shook her head and went to her room.

Her idea about the amusement parks did have some merit. But Dan's gut told him it was the worst of ideas. In places populated by three- and four-foot munchkins, tall, slender, gorgeous Carlie would stand out like an orchid in a field of dandelions. Her very presence in public posed a risk he wasn't ready to take.

All of a sudden, exhaustion swamped him. He'd only slept a couple of hours in the car last night. He didn't dare let his guard down. But now, since Carlie had said she was going for a nap, and since the relief surveillance team was in place, he could barely keep his eyelids propped open.

Dan emptied his pockets on the side table next to the hideous plaid couch, then melted like an ice cream on the sidewalk in Florida at noon. The delicious sensation of a well-deserved slumber brought a lazy smile to his face.

Two hours later there was no scrap of smile left in Dan.

"Where did you go?" he bellowed in futile rage.

Yeah. She was gone. While he slept she'd obviously slipped away. And he'd unwittingly provided her with the means to make her escape. She'd swiped a twenty from his wallet.

He pounded the rickety coffee table, then winced. That wasn't going to help. It didn't even ease his frustration.

Instead of further displays of thwarted professionalism, he chose to put on his shoes, stuff what Carlie had left of his possessions into his pocket, and head out the door. Maybe one of the teams had caught her.

But why hadn't they returned her to the safe house?

He had his answer five minutes later. "Are you trying

to tell me a blond bombshell like Carlie Papparelli sneaked out of that house and none of you saw her? What are you, blind?"

Marcus Tyler and Andrew Ward swapped bewildered looks. "She didn't sneak past us, Maddox. *No one* came out of that house. At least, no on our side."

"Neither one of you had to find a john? You didn't need a soda?"

Tyler gave him a massive grin. "Take a look at our backseat."

Dan did just that, and couldn't suppress the chuckle. "That's the biggest cooler I've ever seen."

"You gotta know Marcie, my wife," Tyler said. "Woman cooks up a storm, and feels her true calling in life is feeding hungry folks."

"What about the portable library?" Dan asked.

"When a guy's just sitting," Ward answered, "he needs good reads. Suz, my wife, manages a bookstore. Her employee discount keeps us in books."

"You didn't get too caught up in the latest thriller and let Carlie—"

Andrew Ward drew himself up to his full, skinny five foot ten. "We *never* read at the same time. Just like we never sleep at the same time."

Dan took a step back. The man's certainty couldn't be ignored. "Gotcha. And Hughes and Rivera said the same thing. They have the rear of the house."

Tyler's grin reappeared. "Sorry, man. Wouldn't want to be in your shoes right about now. It's not cool to lose a subject."

"Gee, thanks, fellas. You're all heart. I suppose you

can take off now. I'll let you know when I catch up to her and bring her back."

The men's laughter followed him back to the front door of the safe house. If he'd been in their shoes, he'd have laughed too. He locked up, then flipped open his phone.

Sonia loved his report, even though she fully understood the danger Carlie faced. "I seriously doubt she's gone for good."

"What if she's turned—this time the other way—and is really gone? What if she's decided she can't put her father and brother away for life?"

"I don't know, Dan. I spoke with J. Z. Prophet about this woman right after I received my assignment. He seemed pretty certain of her integrity."

"She's nuts, and she's lived among mobsters her whole life. Who knows…?"

He let his words die off. The burden of guilt he'd seen upon her last night made him back down. There was no way Carlie Papparelli had cast off her sense of responsibility. He'd stake his career on that.

Which was exactly what he did. "Tell you what. I have a feeling I know where she wanted to go. She doesn't have the money to do what she wants, but she did steal enough to at least make a stab at getting there."

"Steal?" Sonia said. "I gathered she doesn't have a penny on her. She expected to have access to her funds once she settled into her new life. Maybe it was a legitimate need."

He shrugged. "I'm outta here. I have a sneaky subject to track down."

Three and a half even more frustrating hours later, Dan had nothing to show for his efforts. He'd taken a cab to the front gates of both Universal City Studios and Disney World. Needless to say, he didn't find Carlie at either exquisitely landscaped place. And no one working the gates could begin to think back through the throngs who'd passed before them during the day.

His phone rang. "Hey there, Dan," Sonia said, laughter in her voice. "I'd suggest you get back to the safe-house. There's something here you're going to want to see."

No matter how much he prodded, she refused to say anything more. "Nuh-uh. It's too good for me to blow. Get over here pronto."

There was no question that Carlie had done something. What it might be, Dan couldn't start to speculate. Unease landed in the middle of his gut like an overcooked steak. He really, really didn't like the way this had begun to feel.

Sonia's car was parked in the driveway when the taxi dropped him off. "Great. Two of them against me again," he thought.

In the living room, he found the Latina marshal chatting with an older woman. "Where's Carlie?"

The stranger and Sonia exchanged looks. Then the uninvited guest turned and grinned.

"How...where'd you get that get-up?" he asked. "And how'd you get past four experienced agents on surveillance?"

The frumpy Carlie strolled to the side window. "Take a look."

He followed, and noticed the gaps in the next-door neighbor's clothesline. "You stole someone's laundry?"

"Calm down," she said. "I didn't steal anything. I'm about to return the woman's clothes."

"How about my twenty bucks?"

With a flourish, Carlie extended a bill. "Ta-da!"

"So you didn't spend it?"

"No, I did use yours, but Sonia went ahead and did whatever she had to do so I could get my money. She brought me some cash."

He gave his counterpart a sour look. "You're aiding and abetting her. What if—"

"What if you take it down a notch, Dan?" Sonia's voice took on a tough tone he hadn't yet heard. "You can't keep the woman locked up until the trial. You *can't*."

Carlie came to his side. "I know how seriously you take your job. And I know all about the dangers I face. But I can't live like you want me to live. I feel as though I'm choking, as if my lungs can't find any fresh air to breathe. I need some freedom. And I promise I won't do anything stupid."

Objections bubbled up, but he figured it wouldn't do him any good to voice them. Carlie had a point. He wouldn't be able to live in that tiny house, locked away from the rest of the world for any length of time.

Into his hesitation, Carlie added, "Please take a look at me. Even you didn't recognize me. I was careful. I will continue to be careful. But you've got to give me some space."

Dan swallowed hard. "You still haven't said how you got past the surveillance teams."

Carlie grinned. "Easy. I just walked down the neighbor's drive. I don't think they even gave me a second glance. I did good with this—" she gestured down toward her frumpy clothes "—stuff, didn't I?"

"Yeah, you did."

And, as she'd said, he'd put it in very clear terms. She'd hidden in plain sight. The idea of the theme parks looked better every minute that went by.

Now how on earth was he going to admit to her he'd changed his mind?

TEN

"You are now Myrna Day—you should like the name," Dan said. "I came up with it by mixing those of two old-time actresses."

Carlie frowned. "That is the weirdest thing you've done so far. What's wrong with something stupid like Jane Doe? I'd probably remember that better after watching so many TV crime shows."

"Like you said, it's stupid. Myrna Day is at least possible. No one would ever name their daughter Jane Doe."

She collapsed onto the uncomfortable couch. She punched a massive lump at her side. "This thing's gotta go before one of us winds up with a serious injury." Then she sighed. "I guess it's not so much the name that bothers me, it's that I have to take up a fake one that makes me nuts."

"I figured as much. Everyone in your position goes through that same thing. The name doesn't fit, not the person you've been up to now. At this point, you become someone else. The unfamiliar name helps make the break."

That made her stomach lurch. "Who am I now, Dan?"

"Okay. Here's your new bio. And I have to tell you, Sonia and I are pretty proud of ourselves. We did good coming up with the new you."

Another belly bobble. "Uh-oh."

The fiend had the nerve to chuckle.

She groaned.

"Now, now, Myrna. We've been very kind to you. We could have made you any number of unpleasant things, but no. We were benevolent. You're a freelance medical-billing transcriptionist."

"A what?"

"You know. Medical offices hire you to handle their billing. They send you, via computer, the data from their patient visits, and your magic little fingers turn it into bills for the patients and records for the doc's office."

Fear struck. "How am I supposed to do that? I don't even have a computer."

"Never fear. You'll have one by this afternoon."

"And you think I can learn to do all that? Math is stuff you do on the fingers of both hands—you get where I'm going here. I'm no numbers genius."

He sat right on the big, fat sofa lump. "Ow! What's this thing made of, rocks?"

"Now you get why I want to redo the place?"

"I figured that out the second we set eyes on it. But man, this sofa's bad."

Mischief tickled its way up. Carlie let it fill her smile. "I'm not the one who took a nap on it."

His turn to groan. "Don't remind me." He nodded toward the briefcase he'd brought along. "The software you need to do the job is in there. I also brought you the instruction booklet, a start-up supply of billing forms, and a ream of paper."

"What do I need all that paper for? Can't I e-mail or fax the records rather than mail them in hard-copy form?"

"Sure, and that's what you're going to do. But you'll also need to keep records for a certain period of time—and not just computer files or back up disks. Besides, when tax time comes around, you'll be glad you can prove what you earned."

Carlie's head spun. "I'm in trouble. I know nothing about taxes."

"Don't worry. We'll help you take care of that."

She paused to think for a moment. Then that little niggle that had taken up residence in the back of her mind decided to jump forward and make itself a solid concern. "If I'm supposed to be in hiding, why do you want me to take a job? That'll bring me in contact with people."

"You do need a visible means of support. Just think how suspicious you'll look if you don't work but have enough dough to revamp this house, and feed and clothe yourself. All that takes money. You need to have a visible way to make that money."

"But we're supposed to be married. And you're supposed to have a job that takes you out of town."

"Exactly. I'll be gone, and to avoid suspicion, you still should appear gainfully employed. Especially since you won't have kids to watch."

"I guess you have a point. I'd better get busy and study that instruction manual."

"That's the deal."

Carlie took a yellow, legal-type pad and a pen from the briefcase, and curled up with her uninteresting reading assignment. Dan, the rat, dozed.

But then, after two hours of slogging through persnickety details, the doorbell came to her rescue.

The very second it rang Dan leapt up, dragged out his gun, and hissed at Carlie to stay low. He strode to the front door and looked through the peephole. The melting of his shoulders back to their usual posture, the replacement of the gun, the general easing of the tension that his instinctive response had created in the room provided Carlie with fascinating viewing. Dan Maddox in action was impressive indeed.

He opened the door. "It's Sonia."

Carlie brightened. "Hey there, girl! I'm so glad—"

"Okay, you jerk!" Sonia spit out as she jabbed an index finger into Dan's broad chest. "What filthy kind of game are you playing?"

Dan grabbed the finger, with infinite gentleness folded it into her palm, and kept the fist a safe distance from his body. "Hi there, Sonia. It's such a pleasure to see you, and in such a charming mood."

"Quit the garbage. I know what you're up to. And Carlie? You'd better pack up your bags. You're outta here. You can't trust this guy."

Carlie felt the blood leach from her. "Dan…?"

She hated when her voice quivered like that, but the

terror and sense of betrayal that suddenly struck her almost stole her voice.

"You'd better explain yourself," he told Sonia as if Carlie hadn't uttered a sound. He seemed oblivious of her presence in the room. Then that laser gaze turned on her. "*You'd* better not move a muscle."

She'd known fear around him only once before. This was the second time, and her reaction was stronger.

Sonia yanked her fist from his grasp and crossed her arms. "I've been told there's a mole in the Philly office. And his name is *you!*"

Dan's face turned redder than marinara sauce. The tension Carlie saw earlier returned. When he responded to Sonia's accusation, however, it wasn't his anger that struck her; it was his incredible control.

In a measured, quiet voice, he said, "You'll have to do better than that."

"The word is that someone ratted on J. Z. Prophet and David Latham on recent cases. Those cases had connections to your own. Who else would've been in a position to get the kind of information the mob wanted and at the right time?"

"Anyone in the office. And especially whoever stole David's file right out of his office. You should check your facts, Sonia. I've been doing everything possible to keep Carlie safe. If I'd turned, trust me, she'd be toast by now."

Sonia shrugged. "Who knows what your goal might be? You could be keeping her alive for someone—her lovely brother, maybe—to pay you, and then take her out himself."

Bile burned up Carlie's throat. "I don't think Tony would kill me—"

The look Dan flashed cut her words off better than a knife would've done. "Remember that cabin in the Poconos? He wasn't so good at protecting you there. He'd sell you out in a flash—if it gained him something."

"See?" Sonia's voice bristled with indignation. "He even has the right answers. He's the one."

"I am not," Dan countered. "I've only reported to Eliza. You can check my phone records. The only other phone calls I've received are from David Latham and J. Z. Prophet. Go ahead. Check me out."

Sonia sat on the coral-colored cracked Naugahyde armchair in the left corner of the room. "Trust me, I'm going to do that. And I'm starting now. Hand me your phone."

He tossed his cell to her, then sat back at Carlie's side. He took one look at her face, and muttered something under his breath. It didn't sound like a happy platitude.

"Carlie," he said as Sonia dialed a number. "You have to know I'm clean. I've only tried to protect you. You were there in the Poconos. I came to help, not to hurt. I have nothing to do with your 'family.'"

Part of her believed him. The other part didn't know what to believe. "I can grant you that you've appeared very dedicated to my safety," she said. "But I don't know if there's another side to you. There has been to just about everyone else I've ever known."

"Are you saying that even Maryanne is untrustworthy?"

Carlie gave him a sad smile. "Maryanne is different. She was stuck in an awful position, and by your partner, I might add. She's as genuine as a person can be."

"Do you think she'd marry a two-faced creep?" he asked.

"Ah…well, I guess not." His question brought back a number of memories of the other FBI Special Agent, the one now married to Maryanne. "No. I guess J.Z.'s pretty authentic, too."

Dan appeared a bit relieved. "Well, the guy trusts me with his life. Think he'd do that if I was dirty?"

"That does seem unlikely."

"Totally unlikely. J.Z.'s no one's fool. Besides, his father's in jail. The guy was a mob hit man. J.Z.'s got a personal thing against organized crime. He'd have me in handcuffs and behind bars in a flash if he even suspected I'd crossed any line."

"But—"

"There's no 'but' about this. J.Z. and I have worked together for years. I wouldn't be here guarding you if there was even a hint of real suspicion against me."

His voice rang with sincerity, and Carlie didn't want to think he'd faked it. Could she really put her trust in this man? Especially since she didn't seem to have much choice.

Sonia clapped shut the phone. "Okay, so your phone records are clean. You could always have used pay phones."

"I did," Dan said.

Carlie's alarm returned. He had used the phone, but had he really used it to call his boss? She thought back, remembered him relating their Frisbee experience, but then he'd gone silent. What had been said on the other side? Had it really been his boss he'd called?

"Aha!" Sonia crowed. "There you go."

"Yeah, Sonia. There I go. I called Eliza, my boss. Remember her? I had to tell her where we'd ditched the agency car I'd been driving. It would've been worse for me if someone thought I'd done something shady with it. Wanna call Eliza? She'll tell you I called. I'm sure she placed a trace on that call. It's the kind of sneaky thing she does all the time. Even when she doesn't have to."

Then Sonia turned to Carlie. "Did you ever see him use a pay phone? Did you see him meet any strangers? Anything strange about him?"

Carlie took a deep breath. Here it was. She had to make a decision. What did she really think about Dan? Did she believe his protestations of honesty? Or did she go with Sonia and her suspicions of betrayal?

She looked at him, and his blue eyes captured her gaze. The slight tension in his body seemed genuine; she'd be stressed if someone, a co-worker, suspected her of a horrible crime. But his gaze was clear. He didn't dodge her scrutiny.

She remembered his embrace, his concern, his care.

"No," she said, her voice serious. "I've never seen him do any of those things. And I was right by him when he called his boss. Even though I couldn't hear a word she said, his conversation seemed perfectly normal to me."

Sonia slumped back into her chair. "Oh." She looked at the phone and tossed it back to Dan. "Okay. I'll take your word. But you know I'm going to be watching you. I don't want anything to happen to Carlie."

Dan chuckled. "Then I have nothing to worry about. Watch away, *chica*. We're both on the same page."

"You speak Spanish?"

"You know the Bureau wants us to speak more than one language."

"Yeah, but most of you Yankees choose French."

"Sorry. I couldn't do the gargling *r*'s to sound French enough, so I tried to roll those Spanish *r*'s, and guess what? Those I could do."

Sonia winked at Carlie. "See? We Latinos have been right all along. Spanish is an easier language to learn. Everyone should try it."

Carlie chuckled. "I'm a flop at foreign languages. I barely passed my undergrad general education requirement. The two of you can go ahead and chat in whatever tongue you wish. I plan an afternoon with my fascinating manual."

With another wary look for Dan, Sonia crooked a finger at Carlie. "I think you're going to want to put down the books and come with me. I have a surprise."

"Oh, how fun! Where are you going to take me shopping?"

Some of Sonia's sparkle dimmed. "Well, we're not going shopping. The shopping's already been done. But you're still going to like your surprise."

"Can I join the party?" Dan asked.

Sonia shot him a look. "If you promise not to leak."

Dan opened his arms wide. "See? No holes. No leaking going on."

The brunette firebrand shook her head then opened the front door. She gestured with her right arm, encouraging Carlie to look outside. "Ta-da!"

Carlie approached with caution, but then, the moment she glanced outside, she squealed. "Oh! Really? Really, really?"

Dan's hand fell on Carlie's shoulder. "Let me take a look at this surprise."

Tears of joy welled in Carlie's eyes. "Isn't it beautiful?"

Dan stepped forward, looked where Sonia indicated. Then he turned on the petite agent. "What? Are you nuts?"

"Nope. We have to make sure everything looks normal. What's more normal than a plain, boring, beige subcompact in the drive?"

Dan reddened again. "But…but—"

"You sound like a crummy radiator," Sonia said, laughter in her voice. "Something this car doesn't have."

He seemed to deflate. "Fine. But just so you two know—she's going nowhere in that mob-bullet magnet without me."

Carlie's enthusiasm dampened, but only slightly. "Okay. If I have to. But you're not going to like to sit in fabric, paint and wallpaper, and even women's clothing stores. We'll see how long you last on my shopping blitz."

"Hey!" Sonia cried. "Don't forget me. I want to go shopping with you. I want to see what you're going to do with this place."

Carlie grinned. "Wonderful! I'd love a second opinion."

"Er...what am I?" Dan asked. "The proverbial chopped liver?"

Carlie looked at Dan, and his mock-offended expression made her notice again his ability to slip from taut attention to an easy sense of humor with remarkable ease. She'd come to appreciate that quality.

"I'm not all that crazy about liver," she said, "but you can come along. We'll need your brawn—just like Maryanne and I used J.Z.'s strength on our ill-fated shopping trip."

"Let's hope this spree of yours doesn't end up like that one."

"What happened?" Sonia asked.

Dan and Carlie exchanged a serious look. He nodded, and Carlie cleared her throat. "My house got bombed. It's only by God's grace that Maryanne, J.Z. and I escaped."

"It won't happen," Sonia said with certainty. "That car out there's clean as they come. You want a little shopping therapy about now?"

"Let's wait—"

"Let me grab my purse—"

Carlie and Dan fell silent as their contrasting responses crashed.

She sent him a pathetic, pleading look.

He rolled his eyes. "Oh, fine. We'll go shopping. But only for an hour."

"Don't listen to him," Carlie told Sonia. "We'll take as long as we need to find the right color paint and drapes. This naked window's getting to me."

They had a great time comparing paint chips, and

then looking at a rainbow of drapes and sheers. Eventually, Carlie picked a soft gray blue for the curtains in a silky weave, and for the walls all three agreed that they needed to return to the house and check out the paint chips in the proper light. And with the window covers.

So they piled back into the car, and headed home.

But they didn't get there. Not until much, much later.

On the freeway, just miles after they went up the on ramp, the car began to spew smoke. Dan turned to Sonia.

"What's the deal?" His voice had a bite of anger. "I thought you said it was clean."

Sonia had gone pale under her golden-tan skin. "I don't know. The guys at the shop we always deal with checked it out. They're the most thorough people I've ever known."

Carlie looked back at the hood, and the quantity of gray smoke had doubled. "Hey! Could you two hold your argument until later? Much later?"

Dan slanted her a look, then his gaze cut right to the smoke. "No argument. We have to get out of this thing. Something's really wrong."

He turned on his signal, pulled to the right berm, and threw open his door. "Come on, ladies. I want us all at a safe distance as soon as possible."

"It could be some small thing," Sonia said.

"What do you know about cars?" Dan asked.

"Not much," she admitted, her voice sheepish.

"Unless I'm much mistaken," he said as he stepped out, "this car's on fire. I'm not sticking around to check it out, so let's move."

Carlie fled from the ailing car then glanced back over her shoulder. To her horror, she realized Dan had been right.

She watched the hood burst open from the force of the flames. Fire licked up the windshield. In seconds, it spread. The heat grew. Even as they ran in the opposite direction, each breath Carlie took brought in hotter air.

"Thank You, Father," she prayed softly, her legs kicking up their pace as hard as they would go. "Thank You for Your mercies."

She knew. No one needed to tell her.

Someone had meant for her to die in that car. What's worse, whoever that someone might be didn't care that others might have been in the car with Carlie.

Dan and Sonia could have died, too.

The burden of responsibility grew upon her. She couldn't let anything happen to Dan and Sonia. That mattered more than her own life did.

She knew where she'd go once her life here on Earth came to its end. She didn't know if Sonia did.

Dan's fate? She couldn't bear to think he might spend eternity separated from God.

He had to have the chance to meet his Creator. He had to have at least another chance to know the Lord.

ELEVEN

Carlie slowed her pace. She turned, watched the fiery spectacle. "Wow…"

Fingers of flame rose, curled over the roof of the car. Then, with a horrific *whoosh,* they engulfed the entire vehicle.

A hand landed on her back, pushed and sent her stumbling forward again.

"Run!" Sonia cried. "It's gonna blow!"

They pelted down the side of the road, and before long, Carlie heard the now-familiar sound of approaching law enforcement vehicle's sirens. Before she got involved with all these FBI agents and a Federal Marshal she'd rarely given them much thought. Now they represented the opportunity to survive whatever horror had just befallen her.

Oh, yeah. What a life!

Booooom!

The gas tank blew. Carlie tried to breathe, but a sharp pain hit her right side. "Aaaahhh…!"

She bent over, and the footsteps that had accompanied her escape also came to a stop.

"What's wrong?" Dan asked, anxiety in his voice. "Are you hurt?"

"No…stitch in…my side."

Sonia patted Carlie's back. "You poor thing. Your life's become a real mess, hasn't it?"

Carlie gave her a dark look. "You…have to ask?"

Just then, a police car screeched to a stop at their side. Two officers stepped out. Their sunglasses gave them a somewhat sinister appearance. Carlie wasn't sure she could go through her by now one millionth interrogation. She let Dan do the talking.

But that wasn't good enough for Garcia and O'Ferris. Even after they'd verified that Dan and Sonia were exactly who they'd said they were, the two officers wanted to hear Carlie's version of the blazing episode.

Exhaustion overtook her. Her words came out in bursts and spurts. The two cops must've thought her impaired in some way, because at one point, she heard Dan assure them he'd never seen her under the influence of anything but her own nuttiness.

Nice, very nice.

Still, a weak smile tried to break through, but Carlie couldn't dredge up even that much energy. Her eyelids drooped and her shoulders sagged.

As if from a great distance, she heard Sonia say, "Guys? I think we're losing her. She's had a rough time for months now, and it may finally be hitting her."

"Great timing," one of the officers, Carlie didn't

know which, offered. "Fine. Get her some rest, but we'll have more questions for her at a later time."

"Sure. Why not?" she muttered. "That's all anyone ever wants."

"Not everyone, princess," Dan countered.

"I'm not a princess—"

"Yeah, I know. You told me that already." He picked her up in his arms. "Here we go," he added. "Hang on."

Dan's steps rocking her against his chest, lulled her to sleep. She was so tired….

She awoke in a bed. How long had she slept? Where was she?

Carlie sat up, and although she felt okay, she knew time had passed since the roadside interrogation that never was. She rubbed her eyes, focused, and realized someone—Dan, most likely—had brought her to her new little house. It had already become familiar. The bed wore threadbare sheets. Years of use and washing had pilled the blanket to a near tufted condition. Dust and handprints had turned the walls dingy. And who knew how many different pairs of shoes had scuffed the linoleum floor beyond color-identification.

Still, as sad as the place really was, it brought Carlie an odd sense of comfort. It had become her house— well, hers until the upcoming trial. It wasn't her father's lavish European showplace, and it wasn't her late husband's trophy mansion. It was a house—plain, ugly, simple. But to her, it represented a new beginning.

If, that is, her brother, her father and their associates let her live.

With a sigh of resignation, she stood. She had to live.

She really wanted a normal life. For the first time ever, Carlie had a real goal. And what a boring goal it was! Normalcy. Boredom. Grocery shopping, laundry, paint chips, chocolate chips, potato chips and rented videos from the nearby store. Carlie had never experienced the stuff everyone else took for granted.

And she wanted it.

Her clothes were grungy, and with good reason. Fleeing a flaming car had a tendency to soil your garments. An ironic smile on her lips, she went to the small closet and withdrew her other pair of plain jeans and a short-sleeved chambray shirt. The thick-soled flip-flops Dan had bought her in Charleston added up to a normal, boring wardrobe.

Just what Carlie wanted.

The shower helped. Prayer did even more. Reinvigorated, she decided to find Dan and see what kind of trouble had popped up while she slept.

She couldn't imagine there not being more trouble.

"Nothing," he answered when she asked him. "Nothing's happened. Feel better?"

"Sure. Anything would be better than nearly fainting all over you like some Victorian lady."

Sprawled out over the corner of the sofa, he narrowed his gaze and gave her a strange look. "You don't look anything like a Victorian lady."

"What can I say? I resemble whatever that very busy cat everyone talks about dragged in. It's hard for a woman to look her best when she's on the lam."

"Or something like that. It's not the authorities after you."

"That's not what you said earlier. And there are plenty who think you're the mole. It's not even what Sonia thinks. She's not sure you're not the bad guy yourself."

"But you know she's wrong." His eyes begged her to agree. "Don't you?"

His question came across like a plea, maybe overkill, even, but Carlie took her time to think then answer. She hadn't wanted to consider this possibility. She'd avoided these thoughts. But now she had no alternative. She studied Dan, met his intense stare, thought back over the months since she first met him, and then went with her gut response. And a quick prayer.

"I probably shouldn't say this, since it'll probably go to your head, but I don't think you could be dishonest if you tried."

He frowned. "I don't know how to take that."

"Don't ask me," she said then chuckled. "I'm not sure what I know these days. But trust me, it wasn't an insult."

"Yeah, well, I figured that out." He gestured toward the other side of the couch. "Sit. I don't think you're a whole lot more rested than before."

She sat and sighed. "I don't know if I'll ever be rested again. Even if I were to pull a Rip van Winkle, I'd still feel bone-tired."

"It's the stress."

"And the adrenaline I've been burning up is kinda running dry."

Sonia popped into the kitchen doorway. "Doesn't surprise me. And don't think he's Superman, either. He woke up about five minutes before you."

"Whoa!" His aggrieved expression made Carlie

laugh. "You weren't supposed to tell her that. What? You want her to think I was sleeping on the job?"

Sonia's face sobered. "No, Dan. But I'm not sure yet who you're doing that job for. I got a couple more warnings about you. I've been told you've been involved with the cases where the probability of a mole came up."

He erupted from his corner of the sofa. "I told you why I've been on those cases—"

"Sonia," Carlie said, cutting him off. "I know you keep hearing things to the contrary, but like I said, I don't think he's had anything to do with leaks or betrayals or anything like that—at least not on those cases. He's been watching me for a while now, and I've never seen anything suspicious about him."

Dan's eyebrows rose. "What—"

"Let me finish," she said. "He's actually pretty neurotic about my safety. And he's had to come up with some interesting maneuvers to get us out of tight spots. You're going to have to look somewhere else for that mole. No matter what anyone else says."

Sonia's surprise matched Dan's. "Do you think you can be objective? You're too close. It is your skin he's supposed to save."

"I don't think distance is what's needed. I do have the most at stake. But I've seen him in action, not just for me, but to help his partner and protect someone else."

Dan gave a humorless chuckle. "Can you imagine this? An experienced agent in need of endorsement from a mob moll."

Carlie reared. "That's nasty! I can't help the family

I belong to, and I was too young and stupid when I married Carlo. True, I worked hard to ignore what I shouldn't have, but I had nothing—and you know it—to do with their criminal side."

"Yeah, I guess I do know."

His voice lacked much certainty, but before Carlie could call him on it, he went on.

"She hasn't done anything suspicious in all this time, but I can't ignore the need to constantly dodge someone on our heels."

Sonia looked from one to the other, finally staring at Carlie for a few seconds longer than she thought necessary. The small Latina had dark eyes that seemed to bore right through just about anything.

"I don't think he's serious. I doubt he thinks you're the snitch. I don't think you'd put yourself in even more danger." She seemed to come to a decision. "You know, I think I can do more good if I work to smoke out the mole. That way, if it's Dan, I'll be close enough to jump in and snag you to safety."

At Dan's indignant sputters, she raised a hand, palm outward. "Listen, will you? *If,* I said *if,* it's you. You say you're clean, so you shouldn't have to worry. And I'm pretty good at what I do. I might be able to learn more from far away than any of you who work at the Philly office. You might all be too close to pick up on tiny details. That's what I'm good at."

Dan shrugged. "Fine. I'm not worried. I just hate being accused unfairly. But what about Carlie? Aren't you supposed to take over?"

"Take a vacation. Enjoy Orlando a while longer."

Sonia smiled, picked up her bag, and headed for the door. "Just chill, okay? And have some dinner. It's ready. More Cuban food, since you guys liked the last meal I made. The truth will come out soon enough."

Before either Carlie or Dan could say another word, she'd left. His frustrated sigh touched Carlie in a deep, sensitive place. "I'm sorry," she said. "You wouldn't be under suspicion if it weren't for me."

"True, but that doesn't mean we wouldn't have a mole to deal with. It's just as well that Sonia works that angle. Whoever's been ratting on us is working for your dad, your brother, or their friends. Once we sniff him out, you'll be a lot safer—that'll make my job easier."

Carlie winked. "Ah…and here I thought you liked a challenge."

He snorted. "You're a challenge, all right. Now I think you'd better eat. I've noticed you do better with a full stomach."

"Wow, Dan. You must be a favorite with the ladies! What a way you have about you."

He winced. "You wouldn't believe it, but the other guys at the office bug me because they say I spend too much time treating members of the fairer sex to my charming attentions."

Carlie laughed. "You're right. I don't believe you, so I think your suggestion's still good. Let's eat."

After dinner, Carlie curled up in what she'd come to think of as her corner of the couch. Dan went for his. When she'd snuck out to the bank, she'd picked up a stack of brochures featuring the two theme parks she wanted to visit.

She'd only leafed through them, and now wanted to read them more carefully. It took her only moments to get lost in the wonder of it all. The smile burst on her lips without any thought on her part.

"What are you doing?" Dan asked a while later. "I've watched you stare and smile for about forty-five minutes. I'm dying of curiosity. What are you up to?"

She shrugged. "I'm pretty boring. I told you from the start that I want to visit Disney World and Universal Orlando. I still do. These are brochures from the two places, and I can't wait to go."

"There's no way I can let you run that kind of risk."

"You really think walking through a theme park's going to be more dangerous than a burning car?"

"There's a whole lot more ground to secure and a whole lot more people I can't control at a theme park."

"You couldn't control whoever sabotaged the car."

"And there'll be many, many more out in the crowds."

"So? They can get me here, they can get me there, they can get me anywhere—"

"This isn't Dr. Seuss—"

"I know. And I want to live. But if they're going to kill me anyway, there are a few things I'd really like to enjoy before they do."

He didn't answer right away, but instead studied her, a strange expression on his face. "You really do mean that, don't you?"

"Of course, I do. I trust the Lord to take me home to His side when He's good and ready. If some creep decides to hurry my trip there, then I'm sure God's ready to receive me. I'm ready to see Him face-to-face. Until then, I want to visit the parks."

Dan averted his eyes, and Carlie wondered what was going through his head. Had her direct references made him think about God? Eternity?

If so, she couldn't regret her interest in the parks. Yes, it was frivolous, but if her trust in God's provision while she went out among other tourists brought Dan closer to seeing the Father as He really was, then frivolity was all good.

He finally said, "You're not going to let up on that, are you?"

"Would you if you were in my place?"

He seemed surprised by her question. To *her* surprise, he took it seriously and gave it significant consideration. After a bit, he said, "Maybe…"

Carlie knew when she had the advantage. "Look, Dan. It makes sense. Sonia isn't around now. If she's going to go after the mole, then you won't have her help. True, you have your buddies out in the cars, but I'm sure they'd rather hang at the parks than here."

Dan rolled his eyes but didn't say a thing.

"Really. Who wouldn't?"

When he still didn't respond, she went on. "Look at it this way. The people around us in the bus and bus stations made for pretty good cover. Think of the tourists as more cover."

He chuckled and shook his head.

Carlie stood. "Don't say anything yet!"

Thumb and index finger mimicked a zipper across his lips.

She walked to the cracked window and looked out then back at her now-silent companion. "Good. Because it's a really good idea. Think about it. We can hide out at the parks. Well, the park, since we can only hit one at a time."

His shoulders shook with more laughter, but he didn't argue—yet.

She continued. "I'll bet you anything that the massive throngs of Japanese, Indian, Brazilian, German and French tourists will make it easier for us to dodge our pursuers. They won't know where we've gone—*if* they even follow us there."

"Trust me, Carlie, they'll follow—*if* we're not careful and give them a chance."

"Then if they're going to follow us anyway, why can't I see the parks? Let's make use of the crowds, since you're pretty much on your own now. I can't see much of a cavalry on its way to our rescue."

"That's what I'm afraid of."

"So, get smart. Let's do the tourist thing."

He sighed. "In a weird way, your idea isn't without merit."

"Woo-hoo! Faint praise."

"But," he said, "we do have a problem. And it's a big one."

Not now! Not when she'd almost talked him into it. "What's that?"

"You."

"Oh, sure. Blame it all on me."

"It *is* all about you. But so is the problem."

"What's my problem?"

To her amazement, he blushed.

"What's wrong?" she asked.

"Well, you're not like everyone else."

She snickered. "Well, neither are you, Danny Boy. Neither is anyone else. Have you noticed? We're all different. God made us that way."

His discomfort grew. "That's not what I meant. What I mean is…ah…well, you just…you look too much like you!"

"Well, who am I supposed to look like?"

He stood, shoved his hands in his pockets, and paced the room. "Have you taken a good look in the mirror?"

"Every day. Takes some looking to comb my hair, make sure I don't have toothpaste on my chin…you know, that kind of thing."

"You're having fun at my expense, aren't you?"

She howled. "Yep! I figured my turn would come sooner or later. And you're trying real hard not to answer. I wonder why?"

He rubbed a hand over the blond stubble on his head, glared, then threw his arms up in the universal gesture of frustrated surrender. "Okay. You want to know? Well, here it goes. You're gorgeous, and not everyone else is. That's not so easy to hide."

Carlie's jaw dropped.

"Oh, man!" He grinned. "I got you speechless. And I'm going to take advantage of the rare opportunity. You can't go out like…like…" He waved in her direction. "Looking like that. Anyone who sees you stares—even strangers. Everywhere we go. And anyone who knows you, who's looking for you, and sees you, will take three seconds to scope out the situation and snatch you. If, that is, they don't shoot you right away."

An icy shudder ran through her. She couldn't speak.

He could, and did. "You're going to need a disguise. But it can't be anything hokey like that neighbor-lady's clothes. You have to change the way you look a little more radically."

Unease filled Carlie. "Change the way I look, huh?"

"Yeah. That's the deal. You want to go park-hopping, then you have to look like someone else."

She didn't like the sound of that. "Ah…what did you have in mind?"

He shrugged. "Oh, you know how you gave Maryanne Prophet that makeover when we were investigating her?"

She really, *really* didn't like the sound of that. "Yeah…"

"Well, instead of beautifying you, we're going to uglify you."

Groan. "I'm not sure I'm on board with this idea, Dan. What exactly do you want to do?"

"Well, you're a blonde—"

"Courtesy of Santino's gifted colorist," she said, hoping to derail his Pygmalion project.

He stared at her hair. "What *are* you really?"

"Brunette."

"Oh-kay." His eyes narrowed, and he made Carlie feel as though he'd stuck her under a microscope. "How about…"

He stopped and stepped backward a few steps, his gaze never leaving her head. "What do you think about red?"

"Red!" Oh, no. "I'm *not* a redhead. Never been one, don't think my hair'll go red easily, and I doubt it'll look good with my skin."

"Carlie," he said with an all-too-audible truckload of patience and forbearance, "this isn't about a beauty contest or anything like that. This is all about making you look the least possible like yourself. Since you just said red isn't you, then guess what? Red's gonna be you."

Carlie's stomach twisted.

Her palms dampened.

She shivered.

"Are you sure I have to do this?" she asked, her voice squeaky with anxiety.

"Do you want to do the parks?"

"That's not fair—"

"Oh, yeah. It's fair. You want to play, you gotta pay. This is the payment. I'm taking a redhead to the parks."

"A wig…?"

"No way."

Carlie fell back onto the sofa. She thought about everything he'd said, thought back on everything she'd said, all she wanted, what she'd spent so long thinking up. And she realized *his* idea had some merit.

"Okay," she finally murmured, queasier than ever. "I guess it might work. Hand me the phone book, will you?"

"Phone book? What do you need a phone book for?"

"To find the nearest salon."

He laughed. Not a nice little chuckle. Not even a polite, gentleman's laugh. Nope. He roared, his peals of laughter loud and hearty and full of humor. Carlie had to admit the guy had a great laugh, but she didn't particularly care for it coming out at her expense—again.

"Hey, Chuckles!" She stood and waved to catch his attention. "Care to share the joke?"

"Sure," he said between a couple of gasps. "You're the joke."

"Run that by me again, will ya?"

"Carlie. Get with the program. The deal here is to hide you. We're going to disguise you so you can go to the parks. There's no way you're going to pull your nail-salon escapade again. It's a Miss Clairol or L'Oreal night here."

"But I've never colored my hair! I mean, not by myself."

"I'm sure you can handle it. Millions of women do. Besides, the commercials on TV say the instructions are all in the little box."

Panic bubbled up in Carlie. "But what if I burn my hair off? I won't be very disguised if I go totally bald."

"I doubt that'll happen."

Although his voice came out calm and cool, and he seemed collected, Carlie caught the tiny twitches at the corners of his mouth. She also saw his shoulders hitch just a minuscule bit. The wretch was loving every minute of her fear and discomfort.

"Okay, Mr. Secret Agent Man. If you think you're going to freak me out of going, then bring it on! I'll do the color thing. Go buy the tickets. We're going to Disney and Universal."

"First the hair."

"Where's the nearest drugstore?"

"Uh-uh-uh!" he sing-songed. "You're not going anywhere. Allow me to introduce myself. I'm Dan Maddox, personal shopper to widows in the Witness Protection Program. I'll choose the perfect color for you."

Somehow, that failed to reassure her. Nothing about it felt right.

Carlie was afraid. Very afraid.

She had reason. Good reason.

As she soon found out.

TWELVE

"You never said anything about chopping it all off!"

Dan clacked the scissors in his right hand. "It didn't occur to me until I was standing in the hair-care aisle at the drugstore. But then I realized it's necessary. Everyone who knows you knows about your long hair. If we want to disguise you, then we have to do this right."

Carlie clutched the golden lengths she'd dragged over one shoulder with both hands. "Are you sure we can't go for a wig? They make really good ones these days."

"And if you go on one single, upside-down ride? What if it's windy?"

"Oh."

"Exactly. Oh. Allow me the honor of redesigning your mane."

Dan had no real desire to cut off Carlie's hair. It looked fabulous as it was, and he loved how it swung when she walked. But he hadn't been kidding when he'd told her the length of rich waves had to go. Her distinctive beauty was going to be hard to disguise.

The hair, even dyed a different color—Caribbean Mahogany Zing, to be precise—would be in that deceptively simple, and he assumed, exorbitantly expensive style unless they did something radical about it.

For a couple of additional minutes, he watched her struggle. Then she lowered her head. He knew she'd turned to prayer; she did a lot of that. He waited her out. Dan would never interrupt her; he'd come to envy the obvious peace those prayers brought her.

A few minutes later, she took a deep breath, raised her gaze, met his, and nodded. "Go ahead."

Suddenly, Dan's hands went cold. What was he thinking? Could he really put his hands on those beautiful locks and hack away at them? Was he nuts?

His courage took a hike. He wished he were stronger. He wished he didn't feel so unsure. He wished he weren't all alone. He wished…

Yes, he even wished he could reach out, pray, and believe himself supported and protected by a God who loved and guided him. *Believe*…what a word. He wished he could believe.

As he wavered, Carlie reached out a hand and placed it on his. The warmth of her soft, silky skin brought him back to the moment.

"What's wrong?" she asked. "Are you getting cold feet?"

"Something like that. It's just that…well, your hair's really nice, and I've never done this before. You could wind up hating me for the rest of your life."

She blinked. "And you'd care if I hated you? I thought you saw me as nothing more than a pain."

Before he could give his answer a thought, he blurted out, "Sure, I'd care."

"Oh."

This "oh" sounded different from the earlier one. She followed it with the removal of her hand from his, then the turn of her head, and finally the donning of a thoughtful expression.

A certain tension descended upon them. Dan didn't know how to read it. He'd never experienced this much awkwardness around a woman before. Carlie Papparelli was an experience, all right. An unfamiliar one for him.

But he couldn't say it was one he regretted.

And that scared him most of all.

She was getting to him.

"Okay, then!" he said with too much enthusiasm. "Let's get started. Just call me Professor Higgins, and I'll call you Eliza Doolittle."

Every snip of the scissors reminded Dan how far out of his element he'd lurched when he'd concocted this great plan. The only good thing about it was learning that Carlie's hair felt as soft and vibrant as he'd always thought it might. Even if she hadn't been born with the color, its texture and bounce matched her personality. Life and energy radiated from her, and her hair tangled warm and alive in his hands.

Although he still tried to make himself think of her as just another case that had become almost impossible. He cared what happened to her. Not just as a job, not even just for her own sake, but he had begun to wonder what it would be like to get to know her in another context.

What if…?

"Hey! Don't you think you've chopped off enough already?"

He looked down. And panicked.

The once-gorgeous style now looked as though someone had lost control of a rusty lawnmower on her head. Hanks of different lengths drooped every which way, and the shortest bunch exposed a delicate ear.

"Ah…I'm now going for the style of it all," he said, his fear a ravenous force. "I'm trying for an up-to-date Hollywood look."

He had no idea what that meant, no idea what it should look like, but he'd heard one of his sisters say something like that when two of them flipped through a magazine the last time he went home. It sounded good to him.

It clearly didn't to her.

"What's that supposed to mean?" she asked, her voice a high-pitched squeak.

Snip, snip. "Just wait, okay? It takes time to give it shape after I took off all that length."

He'd picked up that gem from a TV show his mom had watched that same weekend. The host had taken the guest through a complete overhaul that had included dumping the poor woman's clothes in a trash can. As a culmination of the experience, the guest had gone from waist-length black waves to a barely there-length platinum cut that looked shorter than his own pre-barn fire Bureau-approved style.

By now, Dan had started to sweat, even though the air conditioner kept the house comfortably cool. Carlie's hair didn't look anything like what that guy on

TV had done to the woman's hair. In fact, Carlie's hair didn't look like anything Dan had ever seen on TV.

Or elsewhere.

Was he in trouble or what?

Come on, come on, come on! He had to be able to do this. How hard could it be? It was only hair, wasn't it? All one had to do was cut it to the desired length…whatever that might be.

The harder he concentrated, the worse it got. Carlie's hair, that is, not his concentration.

She was going to kill him. He considered the Witness Protection Program. For him.

A bead of sweat ran down his nose and plopped onto his left hand. He swiped it off on his pants, and then remembered something else from that bizarre TV show. The hair guy had wet the victim's hair at the beginning, and then continued to squirt it down as he went through his mowing duties.

"Hang on," he said, and ran for the kitchen.

Once there, though, he found nothing that resembled a squirt bottle. So in lieu of the proper equipment, he found a half-empty red-plastic ketchup bottle, squeezed the contents into a coffee cup, rinsed out the container, refilled it with water, and returned to Carlie.

"Ketchup?" Her voice reached glass-shattering heights.

He gulped. "No, just water. I cleaned out the bottle. Don't worry. Everything's under control."

"Yeah, under *your* control. And that's what I'm afraid of."

"I have your best interest at heart." He did, but

he'd never cut hair before, and probably shouldn't have tried now.

He turned the plastic bottle over, and focused on wetting down what hair Carlie had left.

"Aaaack! That's freezing."

He held her down. "It'll warm up quick. Besides, I want to finish here, okay?"

"Don't we have to dye it, too?"

Great! He'd forgotten all about that Tropical Cherry or Caribbean Redwood...whatever. "Yep. That comes after the cut."

"Okay." She sounded skeptical.

Smart woman.

Moments later, Dan discovered that wet chunks of hair were easier to cut than dry ones. So he alternated dousing her with water and relieving her head of even more hair. Finally, when he couldn't find any more disparate-length tufts, he put the scissors down.

"There," he said. "That's pretty good."

"Let me go look in the bathroom."

Panic grew. "No!"

She spun to stare at him. "What's wrong?"

"Nothing, nothing. It's just that I think it'll be better if you see the whole package. You know, the short red hair."

"Short..." He heard her breath hitch in her throat.

He felt like pond scum. Wait till she saw what he'd done.

"Hang on while I mix this stuff, okay?"

He got the feeling she didn't want to look at herself any more than he did. The color better turn out good. Especially in view of the disastrous cut.

In the kitchen, he found a couple of plastic bags to protect the furniture, even though it probably didn't warrant protection. He hurried to the linen closet for something to put over Carlie's shoulders, returned to the living room, spread out the ancient sheet over her shoulders and down to the floor, then picked up his scissors and snipped the tips off the two bottles of hair goop in the box.

"Peuwwww!" Carlie complained. "That stuff stinks. Santino's doesn't use anything that bad. Are you sure you got the right thing?"

He checked out the box again. "Sure did. Caribbean Mahogany Zing. The color looks great on the model. See? Should be pretty good for you, too."

No way would he ever admit that the stuff really stank. He'd *never* let stuff like that anywhere near his own head, so he didn't blame Carlie for her response. But he had to go through with the plan.

"Here we go."

He squeezed the brownish glop all over her hair— what was left of it. The stuff came out thick, much gooier than the separate ingredients had been. Before he'd used up more than a quarter of the stuff, the goop began to drip down Carlie's neck. With his hands in the flimsy plastic gloves that came in the box of hair dye, he scooped it up, scraped as much off her hair as he could, then ran for kitchen paper towels.

The paper towels turned a hideous color. He hoped Carlie's hair didn't look like that once done. He made himself return to the living room.

"Um…this bottle seems to be one-size-fits-all, so I think there's enough here to color any length of hair, even long-to-the-waist. Looks like you have a good coating, so I'm going to put this plastic bag thing on your head, and we'll time the stuff."

"Just get rid of the leftovers, okay?" She wrinkled her nose. "It really reeks."

"Your wish is my command. Don't move a muscle until I get back."

"No kidding! I don't want any more of this stuff on me than I already have."

Dan stripped off the flimsy plastic gloves, and then groaned. A hole must have broken through, because on the back of his right hand, a pinky-maroon stain covered an area about the size of a chocolate-chip cookie.

He squeezed his eyes shut—hard. That better not be what her hair looked like when she rinsed it. It looked as bad as the stuff on the paper towels.

When the alarm went off on his cell phone, he went back and forced himself to smile at Carlie. "Go ahead. Take a shower and wash the stuff out of your hair. Then, once it's dry, you can see what you look like as a redhead."

"What do you mean, I can see what I look like as a redhead? Aren't you going to hang around?"

He sidled toward the door. "Well, it's kinda late, and I'm pretty tired. Besides, you want to hit a park tomorrow. I'm going to need some rest."

"No way." She glared. "I'm not going to look into that mirror by myself. I'm too chicken. You stay right where you are. I'm going to need moral support, Professor Higgins. Besides, I don't expect this'll take long to dry. It doesn't feel like there's much left."

If she only knew…

A short five minutes later, she emerged, a clean towel wrapped around her head. Maybe that was a better idea. Why hadn't he thought of an ethnic costume of some sort? Lots of societies covered their women's heads. And he could've come up with a native outfit that hid her body as well.

He loved it when an idea took shape just after he'd made it impossible to carry out.

The frown lines over the bridge of Carlie's nose didn't bode well for him. He figured he'd better face the music sooner rather than later.

"What's wrong?"

She pulled the towel off her head. Expressions swapped places on her face; she displayed rage and grief with equal strength. "I think you made it shorter than yours was when I met you. That wasn't in the plan. How could you do this to me? What did I ever do to you?"

She fisted her hands, and her whole body seemed to vibrate with her anger. Then she seemed to deflate. "This is…I don't know about this."

Dan couldn't take his gaze from her shorn head. Little tufts of…strange-colored hair rose in every direction, and while she still looked as beautiful as ever, she really didn't look a lot like Carlie Papparelli.

"For whatever it's worth," he offered, "you do look different. I'm not sure you're very recognizable anymore."

"How could I be recognizable? It's weird."

And how! "No…not weird. Kind of edgy, rather. Very young and fresh."

He'd heard that on the show, too.

"Fresh?" She wrinkled her nose. "What did I look like before, a loaf of week-old bread?"

You looked like the most beautiful woman on earth. The thought rushed through Dan's head before he could stop it. He didn't want to think of Carlie that way. And he wondered if his disastrous efforts at altering her looks hadn't been a subconscious effort to make her less appealing to him.

If so, he'd failed. Miserably.

And then he noticed something…really scary. As the spiky spurts of hair dried, the color grew lighter. By now, the tips glowed a weird fuchsia-laced plum. What would they look like when the spikes all dried?

He was in soooooo much trouble.

"Ah…well, since we're done here, and you've survived your transformation…" Dan faked a yawn. "I need to catch some z's. See ya in the morning."

"Not so fast, Secret Agent Man. Join me in the crummy little bathroom. Time to face the mirror—Professor Higgins and Eliza together."

His stomach lurched, and he suspected, for the first time in his life, that he really was a lousy coward. He didn't want to go; he didn't want to face the music.

But he went.

The fat tear that rolled down Carlie's cheek when she got a good look at herself hit him right in the heart.

"Aw, don't cry. It doesn't look that bad."

A sob hitched her voice. "But it doesn't look that good, either."

"You still look beautiful to me."

She turned and met his gaze. "You just want to get out of trouble. But you owe me—big time."

Okay. This was more like the Carlie he knew and lov—

Huh? What was that all about?

Dan shook himself, then gave her a mock glare. "Are you telling me you're going to stiff me on the tip?"

"No tip, buddy. This—" she tugged on a purply-pink inch-long spike "—doesn't deserve a tip. It calls for threats of the most dire kind. I'll come up with some good ones tonight. Watch out, Dan. You're going to pay for this."

His admiration grew. She was really upset. He could tell from the slightly panicked look in her eyes. But she was also a good sport. She was making the best of the calamity by calling on her sense of humor.

Another sob caught her breath. Dan placed his hands on her shoulders. "Hey, I'm really sorry. But I still feel that changing your looks was important. I just didn't expect the results to be so…so…"

"So…punk!" She chuckled. "I've never been accused of being even remotely punk, but I think if we put one of those awful studded dog collar things around my neck, black eye makeup and lipstick, and all black clothes, I might pass for one of those Goth kids."

He squeezed her shoulders gently. "That's a great idea. The two of us should go like that. No one would expect a Fed and a mobster's widow to dress in scary all black."

A dangerous smile curved her lips. "Guess what,

Secret Agent Man? You can't pull off the Goth look with your Goldilocks fuzz."

"No way! I threw out the rest of the dye. There's no way I'm doing pink."

"No, but you'd better come in shoe-polish black. Nothing else will do."

"Is this part of your revenge?"

"Nope. No revenge. Just following orders, sir." She snapped a jaunty salute. "We're going for fully disguised."

He'd set himself up, and he couldn't back down now. "Okay. I'll do it. If you're willing to put up with this, then I can't be any less of a sport. I'll see you in the morning. I'll be the one with the black clothes and the bottle-black hair."

She nodded slowly, and Dan got the impression she'd come close to the end of her courage.

"Walk me to the door," he said, then headed out.

She followed. In the living room, just as he was about to step outside, he noticed the quiver of her bottom lip. He could have withstood all the arguments she lobbed his way, but that silent misery broke through his defenses.

In silence, he reached out and wrapped his arms around her. As soon as he felt her warmth against his chest, he also felt her soft sobs. Unable to come up with words he thought might offer any kind of comfort, he simply held her close. A sense of rightness filled him.

If he hadn't known otherwise, he'd have thought Carlie belonged in his arms. Not just for a momentary comfort either. But it couldn't be. He couldn't let himself think of her that way.

Then she leaned back and smiled at him through her tears. "Thanks."

He couldn't have heard her right. "For what? Making a mess of your nice hair?"

"Well, there is that. But you did it for a good reason. And you do understand how I feel."

A crooked grin tipped up his mouth. "I'm not sure I don't feel the same way. Your hair was really nice."

She gave a brave shrug. "It'll grow back—if I live."

He squared his shoulders. "And that's what we have to keep in mind."

"I'm getting there. I guess you've made me change the way I think."

"Good. Keep it up." He glanced at the clock on the rickety table by the couch. "And it is late. I gotta get some sleep. See you in the morning."

He went to step away, and his reluctance stunned him. He paused. Her hands lay on his forearms, and her gaze lay on his face. Later on, he wouldn't be able to say why he'd done it, but right then, he only knew the pull of the woman in his arms.

Dan leaned down, breathed in Carlie's soft fragrance mixed with sharp hair-color chemicals, but even that didn't stop him. He placed his lips on hers and kissed her good-night.

THIRTEEN

The morning after her Dan-orchestrated makeover, Carlie wanted nothing to do with mirrors or any shiny, reflective surface. A glimpse of herself in one would make her cry again.

She knew it was shallow to mourn the loss of her long, beautiful hair, but she hadn't bargained for such an extreme change. She supposed she would have reacted differently if the choice to change had been hers.

A shower and dressing in clean, all-black clothes took very little time. The Florida heat would be horrible in her T-shirt and jeans, but that was the only choice she had. Toast and tea became breakfast; she wasn't hungry. Even her desire to visit the Orlando parks had begun to dim.

Still, as much as she hated what she'd seen last night, and as much as she knew it would again upset her, Carlie experienced an almost irresistible urge to go look at her new self. Curiosity was a powerful motivator.

Sunshine poured in the bathroom window. The dingy,

cracked white wall and floor tiles reflected the daylight, and she didn't bother to turn on the overhead incandescent fixture. She didn't try the over-the-mirror fluorescent either. They would most likely distort the color of her bizarre hair. She wanted to see it in all its glory. She just wasn't sure she wanted to see it on herself.

Armed with a lukewarm form of courage, she stepped in front of the bathroom mirror, eyes closed. A prayer for strength helped a little, but Carlie had to struggle with her contrary feelings again. Finally, she forced herself to look.

"Aaaack!"

The woman who looked back at her bore no resemblance to the Carlie Papparelli she knew. Dan had got that one right. And because he had, she had to give him credit. He had achieved his goal of disguising her without an obvious costumey disguise.

As always, her eyes glowed large and dark in her face, but in the context of her strange hair, they seemed almost caricature-like. They would suit a toy doll of some bizarre kind just fine. Her skin, in contrast to the dark eyes and weird hair, looked paler than normal. And, of course, the hair…

What could she say?

It did resemble the kind of thing teens and young twentysomethings wore. Because it was so short, no longer than an inch all over, she hadn't seen any reason to use a comb or brush, and it had dried in haphazard tufts all over her head. She was sure some kid somewhere would envy her look; kids used gallons of hair products to achieve the same effect.

But it was the color that really got to her. Last night, in the mellow light of the overhead fixture, she'd read it as a shade somewhere between pink and plum. Now, after a second shampooing and in the harsh light of day, it came across more like an intense shade of lavender-pink.

"Too weird," she muttered. It was the only way to describe Dan's results.

Then Carlie smiled. She wondered how he would react to his own makeover. She couldn't wait until her escort/jailer/protector/tormentor showed up. And not just because she wanted to visit the parks. Jet-black hair on Dan's California beach boy looks? Nah!

Back in the living room, she plopped down on the sofa and clicked the TV remote. But nothing she landed on caught her attention. A logjam of thoughts she'd set aside since last night refused to let her ignore them anymore. She'd done everything possible to avoid the emotional examination she really needed to do. That kiss…

"Lord? What's going on here?"

But God didn't operate on the basis of instant, verbal dialogue when a believer reached out to Him. As new to her faith as Carlie was, she still understood she had to trust her heavenly Father. True, the feelings she had for Dan were frightening. At this time in her life she couldn't afford any kind of emotional entanglement. Especially not with the Fed charged to protect her.

But she'd lacked the strength to walk away last night.

And that posed a problem—many problems. How would they relate the next time they saw each other?

That moment was fast approaching, and she half wanted it to hurry up and arrive, and half wished it never would come.

How would Dan react to her now that they'd crossed that line? Would he still see her as a troublesome assignment? Or would he treat her as a woman for whom he felt…what did he feel for her?

"Aaaargh!"

She laid her head on her hands then went to grab fistfuls of hair, and the lack thereof frustrated her even more.

"Dan Maddox! You're trouble…a pain…a lousy hairdresser—"

"I'm glad you feel that way," he said, humor in his voice. "'Cause this was a once-in-a-lifetime effort."

Startled by his sudden appearance, Carlie rose, and then just stared. If she looked strange as a candy-headed punk wannabe, he could give her a run for her money.

The jet-black buzz-cut look didn't work. It bore a faint green tint that made Carlie think of an oil slick.

"You like?" he asked.

"No!" He looked horrible, even worse than she did.

"Thanks. I'll take that as a compliment." Then he tossed her a white plastic bag. "Here. Put these on. They're the rest of your costume."

Carlie was surprised by the heft of the bag, but only until she opened it. The collection of black leather and shiny steel accessories inside looked lethal. "Not exactly Vogue style, huh?"

He chuckled. "Not exactly." He went to run a hand through his hair, but stopped when his fingers touched the stiff fuzz. He gave her a crooked grin. "Can't say I'm *GQ* material either."

"Nope. You're definitely not."

"You don't have to agree." He winked mischievously. "Gotta tell you, I'm not about to stand here and take such abuse. If it continues, you might find yourself without a date for your park blitz. And that means no park blitz."

She bounded upright. "No way. If I've been forced to undergo this—" she tugged on a shorn lock "—then I'm going to the parks."

"Well, madam, please don your exquisite adornments. I, your humble servant, shall endeavor to entertain you in the best kiddy fun manner."

"Rock on!"

Once steel-spike-studded, Carlie hurried to Dan's new Bureau car.

"Where to?" he asked. "Which park do you want to hit first?"

"Let's start with the original—in Orlando, that is. I want to visit the House of the Mouse."

He groaned. "I was afraid you'd say that. But I am tough. I can withstand inhuman torture. I can mingle with legions of knee-high munchkins and not trample a one."

"You're crazy."

"I aim to please."

And he did. Without another complaint, Dan escorted Carlie through the throngs at Disney World. She'd always dreamed of seeing its many attractions, and that day she did just that.

She sang her way through the It's a Small World boat

ride, let herself be transported back to her childhood in Peter Pan's Flight, admired the beauty of the Magic Carpets of Aladdin ride, and fell in love all over again with the Pirates of the Caribbean. The original ride had inspired the movie, and then the movie inspired the renovated ride.

"That was wonderful!" she exclaimed when, as park employees closed the gates behind them, they found his Agency car.

They both collapsed onto the seats. Dan groaned. "That was grueling."

"Worse than a day chasing crooks?"

"Yeah. That business of avoiding crumb-crushers underfoot takes a toll on a man."

"Give it up, Secret Agent Man. You blew your tough-guy image. You're a softie. I saw you with that little boy who lost the ice cream from his cone. You didn't have to get down to his level and tease him out of crying. And you didn't have to give him and his sister money for re-placements either."

Out the corner of her eye, Carlie caught the flush on his cheeks.

"Nah," he said. "I was just bribing the little rat. I didn't want him to tell that I'd…ah…that is, I wanted him to…er…."

"Yeah, tough-guy. You wanted him to what? Give it up. You can't even come up with a good fib. You just like kids."

"Never!"

"I like kids," she said. "I envy them—the freedom to play and laugh just for the sake of play and laughter."

Carlie leaned back into the car's seat. "So, Dan. Since you like kids so much, how come you aren't married with a handful of little ones of your own?"

"Whoa! That's uncharted territory you've strayed into."

"What? You don't like to talk about yourself? Or is it the marriage thing?"

"A little of both."

Too bad. "So why aren't you married?"

He scowled but stayed focused on the road. "You don't get the hint, do you?"

"That wasn't a hint, Dan. That was a blatant lockout. But you're right. I'm curious and I want to know. Besides, I've put my life in your hands, and I know nothing about you. I think it's only fair if you break down your wall of silence."

"Fair nothing," he muttered.

At first, Carlie thought he would stick to his refusal. But then, when she'd begun to think she'd never learn anything about him, Dan opened up.

"I usually give the typical answer. You know, that my career is too intrusive for a good relationship, that it's too dangerous to force on a wife and family. But that's just a line—true, but not the real reason."

Interesting. "So what's the real reason?"

He shrugged. "My parents and my sisters have great marriages. If I ever marry, that's what I want for myself. And if I've learned anything from them, it's that it takes two dedicated partners to do the job right."

Something deep down in Carlie's emotions awoke right then. She'd never put the thought into words, but what Dan had expressed touched off a longing for precisely that: a partner dedicated to marriage done right.

Dan shot her a questioning look. "You okay?"

"Sure. Go on. Don't stop. You were just getting to the good stuff."

He rolled his eyes. "Relentless, as I've said all along."

"You got it. So go on, Danny Boy."

"Bottom line? I haven't found the woman who fit that description. I don't want a fluffy high-maintenance doll, but I also don't want a grim cause-driven militant of one kind or another. I just want a best friend, a lover, a wife for the rest of my life."

A touch of envy sparked in Carlie. "Lucky girl…"

"If I ever find her."

Despite the knot in her throat, she said, "Keep looking. Don't give up. I'm sure she's looking for you, too."

Only when he turned the key in the ignition did Carlie realize they'd arrived at her Bureau-provided home. She hadn't paid a bit of attention to the ride. She'd been so focused on the man at her side.

The man who, a serious expression on his handsome face, turned his intense gaze on her. "You really mean that, don't you?"

"Yes."

"Thanks." He reached out and took her hand. "And you? What do you want for yourself?"

She gave him a humorless chuckle. "That's much harder, you know. I can't let myself want too much. I don't even know if tomorrow's going to come for me."

His fingers tightened on hers. "It will if I have anything to do with it."

"But Dan, that's just it. There's no assurance, no promise, that you will be able to keep me alive against all odds. Only God knows what's in store for my future. I can sit here and try to figure it out, try to imagine it, picture myself in a wonderful scenario of some sort, but that's worthless. In the end, I have to live each minute for itself, my heart and my hope grounded in God."

"But there's got to be something you want," he continued, dogged. "I know there are no promises of another day to live. But you have to think it will. What would you like when that day comes?"

"*If* that day comes."

He tightened his lips until a white line appeared at their rims, but didn't speak.

Carlie gave him a soft, wistful smile. "You have to acknowledge I'm right. We don't know the future. But I will tell you what I would want if that day comes, what I want right now. I want to be normal."

"Normal? What does that mean?"

She gestured toward the house. "I want that. A little place of my own, days filled with boring stuff like groceries, gardening, trips to the library and a movie every once in a while."

"No family? Kids?"

She shrugged. "Sure, I'd love to fall in love and have kids. But my track record is pretty lousy. I married a guy my family picked out for me. I never even gave him much thought, because our marriage was predetermined. And I guess I'm paying the price for my docility or maybe it was surrender in the face of my father's strong personality. Whatever."

"You can't blame yourself for that. You were raised with that mindset. How could you have thought otherwise? Where would you have learned there was another kind of life out there?"

"The movies. I watched enough of them. On some level, I must have known the truth, but I still went along. I'm not a good choice for a partnership. I'm afraid I would become someone's doormat and let things go their merry little way, right or wrong, regardless."

He surprised her with his laugh. "You're anything but a doormat. I think, deep inside, you knew you'd be risking your life if you tried anything else. Face it, your father, brother and husband are all dangerous men."

"I still come out on the debit side. I was a coward. I could have gone my own way. But I chose the path of least resistance."

"You were just a teen. Do you think a kid has the kind of power you would have needed to survive that kind of rebellion or flight?"

She shrugged. "Beats me. But I was married well into my twenties. I've been a widow for about a little more than a year. It's too late to go back, to try and figure out any of it. All I can do now is my level best to convict them."

"And that's what we're doing. We're a team, Carlie. Let's work together, and I'm sure we can keep them locked up for good. Then you can start to dream."

Tears stung her eyes. "I've never let myself dream, you know? I don't know if I even know how."

He squeezed her hand. "It's not that hard. I'll bet if

you let go of a bit of that control you've put on your emotions and imagination, you'll do just fine."

"But what if…?"

"Don't let the *what ifs* stop you. They'll kill hope and dreams faster than anything else will."

"I don't know if I can."

"Sure you can. And I'm going to help you."

"How? Are you going to dream for me? Live my life?"

"You know I can't do that. But I will make sure you get the freedom to do it."

"You can't promise that. Only God can free me."

"Then trust Him if you must. Maybe…" His face clouded with something Carlie couldn't identify. "Maybe your God can use my talents and training to help you. Is that possible? Would He use someone who can't believe?"

Carlie smiled. "God can use anything and anyone, even an unbeliever, if for nothing more than to show His children how not to be." Encouraged, she took a deep breath then plunged ahead. "But wouldn't it be better if you turned to Him? If you let yourself trust Him? If you also believed, and sought His will in this mess I'm in? We'd really be a team then, a three-way team."

He looked away, let go her hand. "I…I don't think I can."

She took a moment to digest the disappointment. "I guess I have to take your answer as progress. Before this, all you'd say was that you were self-sufficient, you painted yourself like an island. You didn't leave any wriggle room for the Lord to work His way to your heart. But now you just said you don't *think* you can believe. All you have to do is change the way you think."

"You're good, you know? Maybe you should think of a future career as a spokesperson of some kind. You'd be great at it."

"Hmm…" *What a concept!* An idea grew. "You know, if I make it through this, maybe I will take you up on your suggestion. Maybe I will become some kind of spokesperson—but for God. I wonder what kind of ministry He might have for me."

"I can see that," he answered, his smile sincere and straightforward. "I'd say you might want to try something with kids. You have a youthfulness about you. You can enjoy things like Disney World and hopscotch, so I think you'd communicate with kids pretty well."

"It's something to think about."

"And to sleep on." He opened the car door. "Let's get you inside. It's pretty late."

"Yeah, and we want an early start in the morning."

He groaned. "Not again…"

"Absolutely! We're doing Epcot tomorrow."

"Great. More munchkins to dodge."

"You mean, more little guys to buy ice cream for, don't you?"

He blushed. "Maybe."

"You big fake!"

"Good night, Carlie."

"Good night, Dan."

The next day they went to Epcot. They visited the many international pavilions, ate Norwegian open-faced sandwiches, Mexican tacos and snacked at a sushi bar.

Carlie loved the Honey I Shrunk the Audience attraction, although she could've done without the 3-D mice running at her. And Maelstrom, a boat ride through troll-populated fjords, caught her by surprise when the whole boat "plummeted" backward right into the North Sea.

For dinner, she and Dan agreed that Restaurant Marrakesh sounded great, and the scents that wafted to them the moment they walked inside told them the meal would be a delicious adventure.

As she had the night before, on the way home Carlie asked Dan about himself. That night, he told her about growing up in a house full of girls, his skill on the soccer field and his love of horses.

Carlie knew he was creeping into her heart more and more each day. And even though she knew it was the worst possible thing, she began to do what he'd said.

She began to dream.

Of him.

Of her.

Of the two of them.

And the future.

Lord Jesus, she prayed as she drifted off to sleep, *I know this can't be. I'm a killer's target and he's a Fed. I'm a Christian and he's not anything in particular. He has a future, while I have only the present and then eternity with You. Help!*

Trusting the Father for everything, Carlie slept.

And dreamt some more.

FOURTEEN

After Epcot, Dan demanded a reprieve.

"I've done two parks in two days. That's more torture than any man should be forced to endure. Give me a break. I need to recharge, to remember I'm a grown-up."

Carlie looked down at her hands. "That's exactly what I don't want to remember."

"I know."

"You do? How? I never said anything."

"I've come to know you pretty well by now, Carlie. I've been on this assignment for over a year. I've observed a lot of your reactions, your expressions, and I realize that this is all getting to you. Don't get me wrong, none of it has been easy, but all these months have piled up."

She raised a shoulder. "Yeah, but you have to admit I'm a wimp. A stronger woman wouldn't want to skip out on her life and go hang out at theme parks."

"Don't know, Carlie. There were a lot of adults at Disney and Epcot, and not all of them had munchkins along. A vacation's a vacation. Everyone's entitled to take a break from their everyday cares."

"If you say so." Then she grinned. "If that's the case, then why are you putting my vacation on hold? We don't have anything better to do."

Dan picked up Carlie's forgotten manual on medical transcription techniques. "Oh, I wouldn't say that. You have a career to learn."

She wrinkled her nose. "It's boring and dull and confusing."

"But you still have to do it."

"But I don't have to do it today."

"I guess not, but I can't stomach another park. I need more variety in my vacation diet."

"So come up with an alternative, and I'll promise to catch up on my—yuck!—studies."

After a moment's thought, he grinned. "You know? We are in Florida, after all. It's the land of sand and sun. How about we head for the coast and hit the beach?"

"Can we do that? Aren't we in the middle of the state? How long a drive would it be?"

"Couple of hours, but it's early yet, and we can make it there and back in one day. What do you say?"

"I don't know. If you think we can do it, then I'm for it. Anything's better than that booklet of yours."

And that was all the planning they did. Moments later, they hopped in Dan's car and hit a twenty-four hour Wal-Mart for the appropriate beach gear, sunscreen, towels, sunglasses and various other necessities for a day at the beach.

Carlie dozed during the drive. Dan teased her once she woke up.

"See?" he said. "I told you two days of park-hopping were a draining experience. Even you're tired."

"Yeah, but even you have to admit you had fun."

"Fun? It was torture most inhuman."

"And so you choose to spend the day on top of hot sand, under the hotter sun, at the mercy of vacationers? Who knows how many Frisbees will whack one or the other of us."

He flashed her a radiant grin. "Ain't it grand?"

She chuckled. "All right, all right, you beach bum. Didn't you say you were from Pennsylvania? You look like you'd be more at home in California with a surfboard under your arm."

"I wish. I've never gone surfing. But you know? Maybe that's what I'll do once this assignment's over. I'll take a California vacation."

A pang hit Carlie. That vacation would be wonderful…as long as she had him at her side. California held no appeal otherwise.

And she was in more trouble every day. She was no longer falling; she'd fallen for Dan.

She lowered her gaze, curled her hands together, and prayed.

As always, Dan seemed to recognize her need for silence and privacy when she prayed, and he continued to drive in silence. But Carlie didn't resolve her feelings of despair. How could she have let herself care for Dan? She had no future. This was only a matter of a couple of stolen days.

And thieves always paid the price for their ill-gotten gains. What would her price be?

Once they arrived at the beach, she forced her gloomy thoughts to the back of her mind, and let herself enjoy. They swam in the warm waters of the Atlantic Ocean, then plopped down on garish-colored towels to dry off. They'd bought a Frisbee of their own, and they spent a good forty-five minutes chasing after it.

That is, they chased the Frisbee until a sad-looking brown dog got to it before Carlie did. The ratty creature brought the disk back to Dan, dropped it at his feet and stared up, long pink tongue lolling out the side of his mouth.

"Hey, there, fella." Dan dropped to his knee. "Where'd you come from?"

Carlie chuckled. "I suppose you're going to tell me you hate dogs, too."

He grinned over his shoulder. "Nope. I love dogs. Dogs and horses are my thing. But this poor guy looks kinda hungry, and he's dying for someone to play with him."

"How about you play with him, and I'll go dig out that half sandwich I couldn't finish. I know it's not the finest doggie cuisine, but I can't see him turning it down."

"You got yourself a deal." He stood, Frisbee in hand and, with a smooth unfurling of his arm, tossed it for the dog. The pooch went after the toy, but Carlie noticed his slight limp.

"Hey, Dan? See if he'll let you check out his paws. I think there's something wrong with him."

"Yeah, I noticed. He's limping. I wonder if he ran away—"

"Don't count on it," Carlie said cutting him off. "I'd be quicker to suspect an owner who got tired of him and dumped him on the beach."

"You're probably right. That kind of thing makes me crazy."

Carlie unwrapped the remains of her lunch just as the dog ran full tilt into Dan's legs. "Whoa, boy! He's not the one with the goodies." She extended the sandwich. "You hungry?"

The pup ran to her, drool all over his muzzle.

"Here you go."

She dropped the food on the sand, uncertain of his manners, and no sooner did it touch down, than it was gone. It clearly wasn't enough. The dog turned his deep brown eyes up and begged. She broke.

"Dan? Can we go get him something else to eat?"

"You know what this means, don't you?"

"What? That we're going to feed a starving stray?"

"That, and more. If we feed him today, without finding him a home, then tomorrow he'll be right where he was when he stole our Frisbee. What then?"

She tipped up her chin. "You don't think I'm about to leave him here, do you?"

He sighed. "No, I guess I never did. I hoped, but I never really thought you would leave the mangy beast behind."

"He doesn't look mangy to me."

"You ever had a dog before?"

"No, but that doesn't mean I can't tell when one's sick."

"Oh, I guess you're a veterinarian in your free time."

Carlie snapped her fingers. "There you go. That's

what we need to do. Come on. Let's grab our stuff, get him some kibble, and find a phone book. He needs a good checkup, and probably some shots, too."

"I don't like where this is going."

"Well, Secret Agent Man, you'd better start liking it."

"What if he just got loose?"

"Does he look as though someone's been feeding him regularly?"

Dan glanced at the dog's ribs and winced. "You got me there. Okay. I guess we'll play it your way. But we should check the papers. You know, see if someone's advertised a lost dog."

"Yeah, yeah," Carlie said as she threw their belongings in a heap on a towel. "You can buy some newspapers while I'm with him at the vet. Then we can use them if he has an 'accident' at the house. Good enough?"

They carried out her plan. The vet, a lovely middle-aged woman, declared the pup healthy but hungry. She gave him an assortment of shots, even though she suspected he'd already had them.

"He'll want plenty of exercise once the sand-scorched paw pads heal," Dr. Martin said. "He's young and seems to have a ton of energy."

"No problem. I'll put Dan on the job."

"Do you have children? They would help with his energy level."

Unexpected longing hit Carlie right then. "Ah…no. No children. But don't worry. I'll take very good care of him."

The doctor looked at her, questions in her gaze, but seemed to think better of asking anything more. "Here," she said. "These vitamins will help him rebuild his health. I don't think he's been on the beach for very long, but he has lost weight, and I'm sure his nutrition has been lacking."

"I'll make sure he takes them. I'll take good care of him."

Again, the vet gave her a penetrating stare. This time, Carlie had to fight the urge to squirm. And this time, the woman went ahead with her comment.

"You ought to consider having a child. You strike me as having a wealth of love to give. Maybe you and your husband should consider adoption. There are many, many children who need that kind of love."

Carlie blushed. "Oh, Dan's not my husband. He's—"

She stopped. What could she tell the vet? She really couldn't tell her the truth. But she also didn't want to lie. "Dan's just a friend. We were at the beach, and the dog found us."

The vet tried to control her response, but the slight arch of her right brow gave her away. "I see," she said. "You should still consider what I said. And do take the time to find a vet in Orlando. This little guy's going to need regular, ongoing care."

"First thing I do tomorrow morning will be to check out a number of vets. I want to make sure I'm as fortunate with one of them as I was with you. Thank you very much for everything."

When Dan returned from buying a newspaper and a large bag of dog chow, Carlie couldn't meet his gaze. She now felt akward in his presence. Not only had the doctor assumed they were married, but Carlie had also spent the better part of her night dreaming of forever with him.

What was she going to do?

Obviously, nothing at the moment. That is, nothing but get in the car, make the pup comfortable on a bed of towels, and pretend to sleep on the way home. Once there, she'd have to find a way to send Dan away as soon as possible.

But her plans didn't come to pass. At the house they found unexpected guests.

Carlie unlocked the door with her free hand; she carried the dog in her other arm. "Thanks for everything, Dan. I'll see you in the morning, bright and early. Don't forget. It's Universal's Islands of Adventure for tomorrow—aaaah! *Help!*"

She'd never seen a human move so fast. Dan yanked her back behind him, his right hand shot out in front, gun at the ready. "Hands up! I'm armed."

"Ease up, man," said a male voice, ripe with humor. "Put that gun down before someone gets hurt."

Carlie watched the tension drain from Dan. The gun hand lowered to his side, and his grip on her arm loosened.

"What are you doing here?" he asked.

"How about you come inside?" another man suggested.

Carlie knew that voice. She smacked the overhead light on, and ran inside. "J.Z.! Is Maryanne with you? Can I see her? Are you guys here on vacation? I'm so happy to see you."

"Hang on, Sunshine," Dan muttered, sarcasm in his

words. "They're not supposed to be here, so I don't think it's a friendly visit that brought them."

He stepped inside and closed the door. The dog chose that moment to make his presence known with a healthy bark.

"What's that?" J.Z. asked. "Nobody said anything about a dog."

"You have something against dogs?" Carlie asked, her arms tight around her new pet.

"I have nothing against dogs, but I wonder if saddling yourself with an animal that depends on you is the smartest move right now."

Carlie bristled. But before she could say anything, Dan let out a whistle.

"Let's take a minute here, then start all over again. Carlie, why don't you take—what are you going to call him, anyway?"

Carlie, on her way to the kitchen, stumbled. What was she going to call the dog? "Ah…I thought you might come up with a name."

Dan snorted. "You're the one who insisted he needed a home. It's up to you to figure out his name."

"Great." Carlie scrambled through the mush in her head, and found very little there. Then something popped up. "I know! I have the perfect name for him. Frisbee! His name's Frisbee."

Dan gave her another of his crooked grins. "If you say so."

She tried it on for size. "Come on, Frisbee," she said, as she set the pooch on the ground. "Let's go outside."

While Carlie's furred friend didn't respond to his new name, it became abundantly clear that he had been someone else's pet at one point or another. He went ballistic at the word *outside*.

She let Frisbee out into the chain-link-fenced backyard. In her wake, she heard the three men laugh. While glad they could share some humor, she couldn't relax. As Dan had said, the newcomers weren't supposed to be in Florida. It couldn't mean good news.

"You done?" she called out to her new pet. He perked up his ears, gave the ground a final scratch with both front paws, then turned and headed back inside.

In the living room, she noticed that J.Z. had taken the faded coral Naugahyde chair. David Latham, the other agent, one she'd met but didn't know as well, had pulled up a kitchen table as his perch of choice. Dan had plopped into his usual corner of the couch, which left her the one she usually used.

Once she sat, the pup leaped onto her lap, turned one circle, and lay down, his gaze full of love and focused on her.

"I suppose I'm expected to sit here like a good girl, and let the three of you talk. But I'm the hostess—of sorts—and I'm going to get the ball rolling tonight. It's my life at stake, so tell me what's going on."

J.Z. grinned at Dan. "She hasn't mellowed one bit, has she?"

Dan furrowed his brow. "Has Maryanne?"

"Touché!" J.Z. answered. "And Carlie, I understand how you feel. I imagine you know our presence here means bad news."

She bit her bottom lip, her stomach lurched, and she nodded.

J.Z. turned to Dan. "You know what August looks like at the office, with everyone rushing to take their vacation, so I don't need to go into detail about the lack of backup. So what you see here is it. We're your cavalry."

Dan frowned. "What do we need a cavalry for?"

The "cavalry" traded glances. Then David leaned forward. "You're in trouble, man. Big trouble. They're opening an internal investigation into your activities. Word is you've sold out to the mob."

Dan roared an unintelligible sound, and burst up from the couch. "I'm clean, and you know it."

"We do," J.Z. said, his voice calm, undergirded with steel. "But someone's been busy coloring you traitor."

Dan ran his hand over his still-black, too short hair. "And they're succeeding. How'm I going to protect Carlie if the Bureau's after me?"

"Ding-ding-ding!" David chimed. "Give the gentleman the brass ring. You got it in one." He glanced at J.Z. again, and Carlie caught J.Z.'s minute nod. "We've come to think that the mole doesn't want Carlie dead necessarily. But they want her unprotected. The best way to do that is to discredit you, and set the Bureau after you."

Carlie gasped. "But that's awful! Why would they want to ruin Dan's career? He hasn't done anything to them."

J.Z. met her gaze. "He's keeping you from them."

"Sure, they don't want me to testify."

J.Z. picked up a black leather briefcase from the floor at his side. "They don't want you to testify, but I think there's more going on." He clicked the brass lock open and pulled out a fat file. "David and I have spent hours poring over every bit of information we have on your father, brother, husband, and all their associates. Every time we go through it, we land back at the beginning, at least the beginning for us."

David took the file from J.Z. "Dan and J.Z. were assigned to the nursing home case. You do remember, don't you?"

Carlie nodded. "All the old people who died left the nursing homes masses of money, but the money disappeared before the nursing homes could put it to good use."

Dan took a step toward his friends. "Are you saying…?"

"We're saying we have to do the most basic, most obvious thing. We have to follow the money."

Carlie's jaw dropped. Then she pulled herself together. "The four million…."

"Exactly," David said. "The four million dollars they swindled from the old folks and the nursing homes. Where is the money? Who took it? Who knows how to find it?"

Carlie leaped up, ignoring the outraged dog who bounced from her lap. "You don't think I have that money, do you? That I know where it is?"

David gave her a penetrating look. "Do you? Know anything about it, that is."

Rage burned through her. "I never knew anything about my father's—or Carlo's—business. Got it?"

Dan came to her side. "Are you sure you didn't overhear something? That you didn't see what you weren't supposed to see?"

Carlie threw her arms up in frustration. "I know

nothing. Do you think I'd be here, with you as a babysitter, if I had access to four million bucks? Think again, Dan. This isn't nirvana, and you aren't Prince Charming either."

J.Z. cleared his throat. "I think she's been telling the truth from the start, guys. I think she'd have traded the money for Maryanne and her father's lives if she'd had it. And she didn't. Since then, no one's heard a word about the dough. That's a lot of money, and instant millionaires tend to be noticed."

Dan nodded. "She hasn't done anything suspicious since I've been on the case."

"So the money's still out there," David concluded, "but the mob thinks she knows where it is."

"And they want to get their hands on her again," Dan continued, "not just to keep her from testifying, as we thought all along, but also to get her to talk. They think she's sitting on the money, so to speak."

"Wait!" Carlie cried. "It's worse than that. Dan's in danger, too—or so you said. If that's the case, then I'm in danger from the Feds as well."

"Not the Bureau as a whole," J.Z. said. "We don't think you're targeted as such. We think the mole's raised enough suspicion to put Dan square in someone's crosshairs."

"So what are we going to do?" she asked.

Dan placed his hands on her shoulders. "Yeah. What are we going to do?"

"We," J.Z. said, "are going to figure out, even if it's by something as crude and rudimentary as process of elimination, who has turned. Once we know that, we can set a trap. In the meantime, David and I are here to help you—both of you—make it through this alive."

Dan's hands convulsed on her shoulders, his body grew rigid, and his tension seeped into her.

"I don't need the help," he said, his voice soft and determined. "I can do my job just fine. You two need to get back to Philly. That's where you need to figure out who you have to bust. Get the mole. I'll be fine. I'll take care of Carlie. Just as soon as we get out of this place."

She turned, surprised by the steel in his voice, disappointed at the thought of leaving her little house. But she recognized how much greater a danger they now faced. "Dan, don't you think it might be wise to accept their help—"

"I can do my job." Now his voice resembled a growl.

J.Z. approached. "Come on, Dan. Give it up. It's time, way past time. You need help, we're here with the talents the Lord's given us, so don't be stubborn."

David came toward them from the opposite side. "You're a top-notch agent—the best—but you're also human. As independent as you are, what have you accomplished on your own? You're so busy being an army of one that you constantly deny yourself the help and support of friends and colleagues. Don't turn us away. Let us help."

Dan's eyes revealed his turmoil. He didn't speak, but Carlie knew the battle raged inside him. His need for independence warred against the generosity of his friends.

"It's more than that," J.Z. continued. "You have to face the truth. You can't do this on your own. And you need more than what the two of us can give. It's time to look to heaven for the kind of help you really need."

"Oh, stop the religious talk—"

"It's not religious talk, Dan. It's a simple fact. Don't reject the help God offers. He's waiting for you to reach out to Him, to meet Him partway."

A knot filled Carlie's throat. "They're right, Dan."

He met her gaze, and she saw a hint of indecision. She took it as encouragement for her next words. "God loves you, and He wants your trust. He'll be there for you at all times, in all circumstances, in every kind of trouble you may ever face. Give Him a chance."

She held her breath and waited. He'd come to know her over the past few months. He'd also known his colleagues much longer than that. Would Dan take that crucial step and meet the Lord?

What would he do next?

FIFTEEN

As Dan faced his friends and Carlie, he again experienced that longing he'd had when he'd wished he could believe. The empty darkness that met him night after night came back as well. The helplessness of his situation also came to mind.

Mobsters followed Carlie wherever she went. Presumably, him as well. Then, the Bureau he'd served so diligently had turned against him. Someone at the Philly office had gone to a great deal of trouble to point a finger of blame at Dan. Could he fight off all those forces on his own? Could he keep Carlie safe without additional help?

He hadn't argued against Sonia's help because she'd gone to work to unearth the mole. He'd also accepted J.Z. and David's help while they'd been in Philly. They'd also chosen to focus on the mole. Dan's job was to protect Carlie, and so he'd chosen to focus on keeping her safe.

Or so he'd thought.

The so-called safe-house no longer seemed so safe.

The Philly office knew the arrangements the Marshal's Service had set up. They knew where he and Carlie could be found most of the time.

So why hadn't the mole struck yet? If all the traitor wanted was to keep Carlie from testifying, the logical thing would have been to take her out while they were coming in or out of the house. The mole could have done a twofer and taken him out as well.

Instead, they'd experienced relative peace since arriving in Orlando—well, except for the burnt car. But it would appear that J.Z. and David had hit the nail on the head. Multiple motives lurked in the shadows. So how was Dan supposed to do his job?

Could J.Z. and David improve his odds? They were just as vulnerable as he to malicious finger-pointing and murderous bullets.

"Dan?" Carlie said, her voice gentle and encouraging. "Trust in His love."

Something in Dan urged him to take that step, to trust in something—Someone—greater than himself. On the heels of that urge came the familiar need to do things his way, to rely only on what he knew, saw, felt. But, as David had said, what had Dan accomplished on his own? Yes, he'd succeeded at a career he loved, but that career was coming down around him. And Carlie…

He'd envied the peace she displayed in the midst of all the trouble she faced. Would he experience that same peace if he trusted in God?

The longing grew, and Dan realized he'd come to a turning point in his life. Was he ready to reach out to a God he couldn't see, One Who offered strength and peace and comfort? Or was he prepared to go forward alone, to revisit the lonely darkness night after night, to rely only on his own strength?

He reached for Carlie's hand. "What do I...how...?"

She covered his fingers with both her hands. "Let's all pray."

And in that humble, shabby house, Dan surrendered to God, placed his trust in the Almighty Father, stumbled through a clumsy confession, and prayed for the gift of faith.

To his surprise, instead of feeling weak and powerless after his surrender, he felt what he'd longed for. After praying, Dan felt the dawning of peace.

The next morning, Carlie showered and again donned her all-black uniform. She'd never cared one way or the other about the color, but now, after Dan's Professor Higgins act, she'd come to loathe it. She doubted she'd ever wear black again once this whole mess was over.

If it ever was over.

Instead of dwelling on her troubles, though, Carlie turned to prayer, and then, once she'd gained strength from her Lord, she made herself think about the day to come.

She and Dan were going to Universal Studios' Islands of Adventure. Even J.Z. and David had agreed that hanging out at the parks provided her and Dan better cover than staying at the house. It would seem that every FBI agent in the universe knew where she was. That being the case, the Philly office's infamous mole knew where to find her.

Even though she had no idea where her family's ill gotten millions might be found. What had Carlo done with four million dollars? It wasn't chump change.

Carlie sat on the sofa to wait for Dan. Frisbee took the opportunity to jump on her lap. She rubbed the pup's head, and continued to think things through.

Four million dollars…a lot of money.

She remembered her brother Tony demanding that Maryanne, now J.Z.'s wife, turn over the money in exchange for her father's life about a year ago. She, of course, had known nothing about the loot. Neither had Carlie, but Tony hadn't believed them. Carlo must have hidden the money to keep Carlie's father, brother and any of their cronies from getting their hands on it.

Carlo hadn't meant to die, but he had, and all for money.

"Penny for your thoughts?" Dan asked as he sat at her side.

"How do you always manage to surprise me like that? I never hear you when you get here."

Dan blew on the fingernails of his right hand then buffed them on his shirt. "Years of training."

"I guess." She shook her head. "I'm trying to figure out where all that money might have gone. I only know there isn't that much in my account—sure, it's healthy, but not to the tune of four million dollars."

"Trust me, if those millions had been there at any time, you wouldn't be out and around. We'd have locked you up right away."

"Comforting feeling."

"Did all that thinking get you anywhere?"

"Do you mean about the money?" When he nodded, she went on. "No. I have no idea what might have happened."

"Then it makes no sense to keep churning it over ad nauseam." His expression turned hopeful. "I don't suppose you've changed your mind about the park?"

She put Frisbee on the floor and stood. "Not a chance, Special Agent Man. You and I have a date with a park."

After a brief disagreement about Frisbee—Carlie had no intention of leaving her new pet behind, while Dan had no intention of bringing the dog along—the three of them got in Dan's car, and drove to Islands of Adventure.

Fortunately for Carlie and Frisbee, the park offered dog-sitting services. Once they'd settled her baby in his temporary quarters, Carlie and Dan headed out to enjoy the park.

Again, Carlie loved every second of her day. She laughed through the Amazing Adventures of Spider Man, a 3-D ride through city streets that also included a flight among high rises and over a variety of stores. The highlight of the ride was the four-hundred-foot free fall. Carlie felt she'd experienced the same thrills and chills as Spidey might have.

At lunch, she caught Dan staring at her. "What? Do I have mustard on my chin?"

He shook his head. "I can't get over how little attention your choppy lavender hair seems to draw."

She scoffed. "Have you bothered to look around? See how many kids have weird-colored hair? And there's a bunch of them with these awful leather and steel things."

Dan laughed. "What? You don't like the jewelry I bought you?"

"Spare me! I've never been a bling-freak, but this is so far out of the realm of jewelry that it doesn't even deserve the name." Then she nodded toward his black-dyed, fuzz-covered head. "And how about you? You fit in with some of the stranger ones."

He patted the top of his head. "I can't believe they actually do this by choice."

"You mean you don't like your new style?" she asked, tongue in cheek.

"Gack! The goop I have to use to keep it like this itches. I can't wait to wash the stuff off every time you make me wear this awful costume."

"What do you mean, *I* make you wear it? You're the one who came up with the idea."

"Yeah, but you're the one who wants to hit every park in town."

"Which reminds me…are you done with that hot dog?" When he nodded, she continued. "Come on. The day's wasting, and there are plenty more attractions to see."

She made him go through the *Jurassic Park* River Adventure boat ride four times with her. She got a kick out of being chased by hungry T rexes.

"Sick," Dan said, shaking his head. "But I hope you've had enough now. I'm ready to go home."

"You know, I am, too. Let's go get Frisbee and head back."

This time, Carlie really fell asleep, Frisbee curled on

her lap. When they pulled up into the driveway, she awoke and yawned. "I'm ready to hit that pillow. I'm beat."

"Phew!" he said. "I was afraid you'd say you wanted to do another park in the morning."

"But I do! I left the best for last. Universal Studios Florida is for tomorrow. That's the one that is an actual film and TV studio, plus they have a bunch of rides and attractions, too. Besides, you promised we'd eat at Emeril's when we went back."

"Okay, okay. I promised. We'll eat at Emeril's tomorrow. Now let's get you both inside."

But no sooner did they step in than they both knew this was the last time they would do so.

"Get in the car!" Dan cried, gun in hand.

She didn't argue. "Come on, Frisbee!"

To her amazement, the puppy obeyed. Dan, however, went into the trashed house. "What are you doing? What if they're still inside?"

"That's why you're there, I'm here, and I have a gun."

"But—" She stopped when he disappeared into the little house. It really hit her hard. She'd liked the house; she'd especially loved thinking up the changes she'd planned to make. But she should have known it wouldn't come about. She didn't have a future, not unless her family and all their colleagues were locked up behind bars. How unreasonable was that?

So…what next? Where were they going to go?

"You'd better not even think of calling this in to your boss," Carlie said when Dan returned, a grim look on his face.

"Don't worry. She's on vacation. I'm not calling

anyone, especially since I think the office phones have been bugged. At least, hers must have been. Otherwise, I don't know how the mole gets his data."

"Are you sure it's the office phone that's bugged? Couldn't it be your cell phone that's being tapped?"

"I don't know much about the technology, but I don't think so." He took out the silver device, turned it over and over in his hands, then dropped it on the dashboard. "Just in case, I'm not going to use it. But I don't think that's how they were listening. Maybe the house…"

A tear rolled down Carlie's cheek. "I really liked the house."

"I know. And we'll find you another one, a better one. I promise."

"Don't promise, Dan. You might not be able to keep it."

"True, but I'll do my best."

"I know."

Neither spoke for minutes, and aside from Frisbee's gentle snores, nothing disturbed the silence. Then Carlie couldn't stand it anymore. "So what are we going to do next? We can't just stay here."

He turned the key in the ignition. "Let's go meet up with David and J.Z."

A short half-hour later, they met at an all-night family-style restaurant. Over endless cups of coffee, they went over every detail they knew. Every page in the file came in for its fair share of examination, and every possible idea was taken apart bit by bit.

Nothing. They came up with a big fat nothing. And Carlie was falling asleep.

Then J.Z.'s phone rang. From his side of the conversation, she gathered Maryanne, his wife, was on the other side. Carlie missed her friend, and she wished she dared ask for a chance to talk to her, but she didn't feel she should interfere.

Then J.Z. surprised her. "Want to talk with Maryanne? I know she'd love to hear from you."

Tears of joy poured down Carlie's face. She grabbed the phone, and relished the sound of her friend's voice. "I can't believe it's really happening! I didn't think I'd ever have another chance to talk with you. You know, that Witness Protection deal is pretty grim."

Then Maryanne surprised her. "Listen," she said, "I didn't say anything to J.Z., but…"

And they talked. Carlie laughed and cried. Then, in a much better mood than before, she eventually hung up, and handed the phone back to J.Z.

"Thanks."

"Are you kidding?" Dan's partner said. "She would've had my head on a platter if I hadn't given you the phone. She's spent the last few months worried sick about you."

Carlie shrugged. "I'm fine…I guess."

And then, when none of the men expected it, Maryanne Prophet and another woman ran up to their table. This time Carlie couldn't stop the flow of her tears.

J.Z.'s frown, however, was something to fear. "What are you doing here?"

Maryanne wrapped her arms around her husband's neck. "If you can take an Orlando vacation, then so can we."

Carlie looked through her tears and saw the other woman, a pretty blonde, lean over and kiss an unhappy David. She turned to Dan, and gave him a questioning look.

"That's Lauren DiStefano," he said. "She's David's fiancée. They're planning a Thanksgiving wedding."

Maryanne gave J.Z. a gentle shove. "Move over. There's plenty of room on the booth bench." Then she glanced at Carlie. She frowned. "Who's she—"

The new Mrs. Prophet brought her words to an abrupt end. She gaped. "Carlie? Is that really you? What happened to your hair? You look…well, you don't look…I mean…"

"It's okay," Carlie said with a sobbing laugh. "I know I look awful, but it's okay. It's my disguise."

Maryanne narrowed her eyes. "And whose idea was that?"

Carlie laughed. "Trust me, it wasn't mine."

Dan cleared his throat. "Uh…it wasn't supposed to turn out lavender. It was supposed to be kind of dark red."

From that point, the conversation lightened up. But Carlie suspected that when J.Z. and Maryanne, and David and Lauren, had moments alone, sparks would fly between the two sets of partners. The men weren't happy about the women's presence in the middle of a case.

Then, after they'd laughed and talked and munched on a variety of goodies they'd finally broken down and ordered, an idea began to take shape in the back of Carlie's mind. The more time that went by, the clearer it grew. She lost track of the general conversation.

And even though she suspected the others thought her silence sprang from simple exhaustion, Carlie believed she'd figured out at least one part of the puzzle. When she caught Dan's gaze on her face, she gave him a tentative smile.

"Are you okay?" he asked.

"Yeah…" She drew out the word. "I think I'm more okay now than I've been in a while."

"I'll bet you're thrilled to see Maryanne."

"That too."

"Too?"

"Yes. Dan?" Even though Carlie was sure of her deduction, she felt awkward offering her theory to a man who made a living figuring out the workings of the criminal mind. "I have an idea. About the money."

He leaned closer. "The money? You mean, the four million?"

She nodded. "I think I know where it is."

His blue eyes did their laser impersonation, and his stare seemed to probe every corner of her thoughts. "Well?" he asked. "Are you going to let me in on your newest secret?"

After a deep breath, Carlie shrugged. "I think I finally know the reason for that empty casket they shipped to Sicily."

Dan blinked. Then he gave the concept some thought. After a few silent minutes, he let a smile curve his lips. "What was that line of Professor Higgins? 'She's got it. I think she's got it!'"

Carlie smiled in relief. She'd been afraid he'd think her idea stupid. "You agree?"

With a nod, Dan turned to the others. "Hey, guys? Do either of you know what happed to Carlo's empty casket? Did Interpol return it to our office? We'd better find it, and quick. I'm willing to stick my neck out here, but Carlie just figured things out. I'm going with her theory. Don't you think all that cushy silk padding, not to mention thick lead casket walls, is a perfect hiding place for…oh, just about four million smackers?"

Lauren leaned forward. Then she reached for David's hand. "Do you think…would there be room for about a million more?"

Carlie gasped. "More? More missing money?"

David turned to face her. "Before he faked his death, Lauren's brother did a nice business investing dirty money for some nasty characters. That money's missing, too."

"And you think Carlo had something to do with it?"

Lauren nodded. "His name appeared on some of Ric's papers. I think we—you—figured it out."

Carlie dropped back against the puffy booth cushion. "You gotta admit, hiding all that dough in an empty casket was pretty creative."

Dan began to hum the song about the rain from *My Fair Lady*. "She's got it!" he exclaimed. "By George, I think she's got it."

SIXTEEN

"That's all great," Carlie said after they'd discussed every possible angle on the money and its probable hiding place. "But my safe-house is no longer safe. What am I supposed to do tonight? Where are Frisbee and I going to bunk down?"

The dog, who'd been left asleep in Dan's Bureau car, was an issue. Where would she and Dan keep him? The two of them might bounce from motel to motel—there were plenty of them in Orlando—every other night, but what were they going to do with the dog? Few, if any, motels allowed pets.

The kennel at the Universal Studios parks would let her keep Frisbee there only during the day. Then she remembered a notice she'd seen near the entrances of the two Disney parks. There, boarding kennels welcomed pets overnight. But Carlie wasn't visiting Disney again. She'd been to those parks, and she doubted she could talk Dan into taking her back. Besides, she really wanted to see the Universal Studios' attractions, especially the TV and film studios inside the parks.

Why couldn't she board Frisbee at Disney, and then visit Universal? Would Dan put up with all that driving around?

Then Carlie grinned. Did he have a choice? They had the dog, they had to evade bad guys and misguided good guys, and a pup would get in their way. They did have to sleep somewhere.

"What's that grin for?" Dan asked, leaning close.

"I figured out what we can do with Frisbee," she said in a quiet voice.

"Uh-oh. I'm afraid. Hit me with this idea—gently."

"Hey! It's a good one." She glared. "And you're not going to get out of taking me to Universal tomorrow just because we have to find a place to keep my pooch."

He looked sheepish. "Okay, so what do you want to do with him?"

"Frisbee's going to Disney!" His look of bewilderment made her laugh. "No, I'm not crazy—at least, not so much. The Disney parks have nearby boarding kennels that keep animals overnight. Universal's does not. All we have to do is leave my pooch at a Disney kennel. I would still want to spend time with him every day."

Dan stroked his chin. "I guess that might work."

"What would work?" asked David.

"Parking Carlie's dog at the Disney kennel while I take her touristing again tomorrow."

"Touristing?" Maryanne wrinkled her nose. "That's not a real word, Dan."

"I know, Madame Librarian. I made it up, you got the picture, and it got the discussion where I wanted it to go."

"Where's a good thesaurus when you need one?" Maryanne quipped.

"Uh…hello?" Carlie broke in. "What about me? Us? Where do we sleep?"

J.Z. and David looked at each other. J.Z. turned to Carlie. "I would suggest our motel, but I'm afraid the mole would track this large a bunch of us much faster than if we just got a room for you—even a room for Dan, too. Two people are easier to hide than six."

Carlie nudged Dan so she could leave the booth. "So what are we waiting for? This city's nothing if not a hotel boon. I'm tired, and I want to hit the park in the morning."

Maryanne looked surprised. "Are you nuts? It's two o'clock already, and there are crazy people out there who want to kill you. Why don't you just stay out of sight and plan to take it easy tomorrow?"

"Visiting the park *is* taking it easy. Besides, I'll be out of sight in the middle of the crowds at the park." Carlie then turned to Dan. "Do you think Frisbee will be okay in the car all night?"

Dan rolled his eyes. "I told you the dog wasn't a good idea for a woman on the lam. I suppose he'll be fine if we provide him with plenty of water, keep the windows cracked open, and go get him very early before the heat rises…. Oh, forget it. I'll just sleep in the car with him."

"Oh! But that's not fair on you." Carlie frowned. "Maybe I should sleep in the car with Frisbee. He is my dog, after all."

J.Z. snorted. "All right, already. This is the way it's going down. I'm the senior agent here—"

"But it's my case," Dan argued.

"Since I'm the senior agent here," J.Z. said again, as if Dan hadn't spoken, "Maryanne will use my motel room, Carlie can use the second queen size bed there, and Lauren can use David's or get another room. David, Dan, and I will stay in the car with Frisbee, and we can take turns on surveillance duty."

Dan and David groaned. The three women chuckled.

"So when do we get to go across the street?" At the end of Carlie's question, she had to cover her mouth to stifle a yawn.

Dan slapped the tabletop, and then stood. "Okay, folks. We have a plan. I'm not crazy about it, but we have a plan."

And for the night, the plan worked. The next day, everyone agreed that a trip to Universal Studios made sense. There was some safety in numbers, and should anything happen, having three agents on the park grounds was better than if they had only one.

They wouldn't go as a group, of course, and so Dan and Carlie left first. They boarded Frisbee at the kennel then went to indulge Carlie's theme-park appetite.

They crossed paths with David and Lauren on the *Jaws* boat ride. Both couples boarded the same boat, took the ride through the well-depicted New England set, and just when Carlie relaxed, a fin sliced through the water and they faced the gaping maw of the rapacious great white—Jaws.

Later, in line for the Earthquake attraction, Carlie and Dan made sure they gave no indication that they knew J.Z. and Maryanne. All four entered the venue, and the women shrieked as ceilings collapsed, subway cars crashed, and gasoline trucks exploded. Afterward, everyone felt they'd experienced an authentic 8.3 Richter scale quake.

After they'd exhausted the variety of rides and attractions, including the studios Carlie wanted to visit, she and Dan left the Universal Studios grounds, ready to spend time with Frisbee. Tired, they decided to call it a day, even though the park still hadn't closed the gates.

As they headed for Dan's car, however, they noticed a shadow on the right side of the vehicle. A shadow, human in shape, but with no person near enough to cast it. Then the shadow moved, its actions stealthy, quick.

Dan grabbed Carlie's hand. "Wait!"

"I see him."

He nudged her. "Go back! David and J.Z. haven't left yet. They were going to wait until we drove away before following. Go find them."

"Alone?" Carlie's voice came out like a squeak. She tried again. "Without you? And leave you alone?"

"Shhh! Just go! This is my job, Carlie. I know what to do."

"Yeah, like you'll know what to do with a hole in your gut if he greets you with a bullet."

"So what good will it do if you get a shot in the gut, too?"

She tugged on his arm. "Then you have to come with me."

"I want to get this guy. Would you just go? Before we catch his attention?"

"If you come with me, we won't draw his attention.

And if we can find David and J.Z., then maybe the three of you can catch him, and no one gets hurt."

"I can do my job, Carlie. I don't need help from anyone else—"

"Dan! You need God's help. Don't try to go it alone anymore. Remember, you took a big step toward Him. He's there for you, no matter what." She turned her hand, laced her fingers through his, and squeezed. "Let's pray."

For a moment, she feared he'd argue. Then he gave a slow nod and bowed his head. They sought the Lord, asked for wisdom and courage and strength. They asked for insight, for protection, and for the truth to come to light.

Before they reached their amens, however, David's arrival from behind startled them. Dan spun, crouched, pulled his gun.

David grabbed his friend's hands, turned the gun skyward. "Easy," he said. "It's just me. We saw you two hiding, and we couldn't figure out what you were doing. What's up?"

Dan's whisper came out rough. "Over there. By my car. We saw a man's shadow."

David jerked his head toward the park gates. "Let's go. Let's get back to the others. We can meet up somewhere and come up with something."

Dan glared. "But he'll get away—"

"So will you two—with your lives."

Carlie watched Dan struggle with his independent nature and the wisdom of David's suggestion. She offered a silent prayer for Dan, and thankfully, saw him nod after a minute or two. All three slipped back through the gates, one at a time.

Once inside the confines of the park, Dan and David agreed that Carlie should head for the ladies room. They would send Maryanne and Lauren who'd use the door at the facilities' opposite side.

The three women huddled together, and using J.Z.'s brand-new, just-purchased-that-morning set of walkie-talkies, the six discussed the situation, possible solutions, and speculated as to the identity of their "shadow." Dan and Carlie couldn't return to the car, much less to the motel. Suggestions flew back and forth, but nothing definite came of the discussions.

"How about…" Carlie started, then stopped. It was a crazy idea. No one else would likely go along with it. But what could it hurt to suggest it? "What if we stayed in the park overnight?"

The two other women stared at her. Initially, both wore puzzled expressions. Then Lauren began to nod.

"That's not a bad idea," she said. "They have security here, lots of empty buildings—dark and empty except for whatever maintenance crew shows up. You should be able to avoid them."

Carlie heard a male voice squawk over the gadget in Maryanne's hand. "Who's that? And what's he saying?"

Maryanne handed her the device. "It's Dan, and either he heard your idea or he heard you had one. Go ahead. Tell him. For what it's worth, I think it'll work."

Fortified by the others' favorable opinions, Carlie took the walkie-talkie. "Dan, I know you're going to think I'm crazy—"

Loud squawks assured her he didn't just think she was crazy; he was certain of her insanity.

"Come on. Listen to me. Maryanne and Lauren agree that my idea will work."

He squawked some more about letting him make up his own mind, and then he urged her to tell him what she'd come up with. "Well," she started, "the park is big, dark, and has a pretty good security detail, doesn't it?"

"I don't like where you're going—"

"Give me a chance, okay? I don't think Lauren or Maryanne are particularly crazy or thrill-seeking risk-takers, and they agreed with me. It would make sense if we stayed in the park and hid in one of the dark, empty attractions."

"That's nuts."

"No, it's not. Where else are we going to go? We don't have transportation now. We can't involve David, J.Z., Maryanne and Lauren any more than they already are. So what else do you suggest? And don't you think your partners should be looking for the mole instead of following us around?"

She heard him draw a deep breath. "First you think there's safety in numbers. Now you think we need to go it alone. Make up your mind, will you?"

"Does that mean you're going to do it?"

His exhalation spoke of exhaustion and frustration. "It means I'm tired, and don't have many options left. I'll run your idea past the guys. And you do have a point about the mole. Either J.Z. or David should check in with Sonia. I haven't heard back from her in days."

The walkie-talkie sputtered silent, and Carlie turned to her companions. "I think you'd better get going. The park's about to close, you don't want to get locked up in here with us—it would be too suspicious. Besides, Dan's going to need help talking the other two into my idea."

Lauren smiled. "I think you're right. We'll go, but be careful."

Carlie watched the women leave, her apprehension growing. Was she crazy or what? Trying to avoid killers by spending the night in a theme park was kind of out there. For all she knew, the maintenance crews might have more members than the throngs of tourists that visited each day. That would make it even harder for them to stay hidden.

But…didn't everyone around this park wear a uniform of some kind? Maybe the maintenance people did, too. Maybe she and Dan could get hold of uniforms. Nah, that would never work. Better to stick with the all-black look. They could hide in the shadows.

As time passed, Carlie grew more apprehensive. Where were the others? What had they decided? What were they going to do with her? They didn't expect her to spend the night in a bathroom, did they?

Lord, help! Help us through this. Guide us, lead us to… I don't know. Wherever You want us. And be with Dan. He's not sure of You yet. Help him see Your hand in all that happens next.

"Psst!"

Carlie jerked with shock. "Can't you warn me before you scare me to bits?"

Dan chuckled. "Do you know how crazy that is?"

She shrugged. "What do you expect? You scare a woman's socks off, and you have to figure she won't be too coherent right after. Where were you?"

"I was making plans with the guys. Where'd you think I was?"

"Beats me, but time sure slows down when you're all alone in an empty bathroom. Especially when you know some creep's out to get you."

Dan shook his head. "Come on, you nut. We're not spending the night here."

"Any chance for a couch? Pillow? Even a carpeted floor will do."

"I think we can provide at least one of those amenities."

"That's right. You've said it before. You aim to please."

A strange expression softened his features. If Carlie had to guess, she'd say it was wistfulness she saw. But that was strange, certainly in a strong man like Dan.

"Penny for your thoughts?" she asked, turning the tables. The last time she'd heard those words, he'd asked them of her.

"Just a thought. I really do aim to please. It's not just a phrase. I really like to see you smile."

"Oh!" Carlie blushed. What a nice thing he'd said. She was about to tell him, when she realized his admission had embarrassed him. Could he care for her more than he let on? Had that kiss meant more than a casual caress to him, too?

What a time and place for a thought like that! Carlie shook herself, gave Dan a bright smile, and then said, "Give me a minute to wash my face. I'm feeling pretty gross after a day in the hot sun."

"Go ahead."

Carlie cupped her hands under the faucet then splashed her face with the cool water. A dot of liquid hand soap from the dispenser frothed between her fingers, she rubbed it over her cheeks, cringed at the slight stinging sensation, then rinsed, and grabbed a wad of paper towels from the dispenser.

"Boy, these feel like sandpaper." She dumped the offending damp paper in the trash. "I miss my lotions and potions."

Dan chuckled. "Girly girl."

She gave him a mock scowl. "What are you waiting for? You don't expect me to stay in a bathroom all night, do you?"

"I said we weren't going to stay here a moment ago. Did you forget?"

With thoughts like the ones she'd tried to forget by washing her face, sure! She was likely to forget just about anything. "Something like that. If we're going, then let's go. Do you have any idea where we're going?"

"Beats me. It'll be an adventure. Let's keep an eye out for the maintenance crew. Maybe we can get into one of those buildings. Many of the enclosed attractions had carpeted floors."

"And some had upholstered seats."

"We'll have to be careful. This is trespassing— against the law, you know."

"So is killing us, Dan. Where else are we going to go?"

"I'll come up with something," he said, "but I'm

nearly sleepwalking, I'm so tired. Come on. Let's go see what we can find."

Carlie noticed the slump of his shoulders. He hadn't exaggerated; he was tired. She felt an urge to wrap her arms around him, to comfort him, to help him find rest, but she knew she couldn't. Still, the urge remained.

They began to retrace their steps of earlier in the day. As they slipped from shaded storefront to shaded storefront, the altered mood of the park struck Carlie. She shivered. "Isn't it weird?"

"Weird?" Dan asked. "It's just empty and dark."

"Yes, I know. But doesn't it look eerie, almost as if the shadows are full of secrets. It feels as if those secrets might come alive at any moment."

When they arrived at the street corner, Dan paused in a darkened doorway. He looked both ways, behind them, up ahead, checking out what Carlie assumed would be their next hiding place. The breeze whistled through the canyon created by the tall building fronts. Hairs at the back of her neck rose at the sound of the wind. "It's so eerie. What's hiding out here with us?"

"Isn't running from the mob bad enough?" Dan said in a grumpy voice. "Do you have to imagine bogeymen in every corner?"

"I don't imagine them. They're there. Evil has been chasing me long enough that I know I can't escape it— not really. I can only pray that the Lord will keep me alive long enough to help bring that evil to justice."

"I'm not even sure it's your family's pals who are after us. At least, not right now. I suspect the mole more than I do them. What I don't understand is his motive."

Carlie studied the empty street again. The building fronts rose on either side, three stories tall some of them. The colorful façades appeared strong, sturdy, as if they'd stood there for years. But Carlie knew the reality behind the fronts. Operations centers hid back there, systems that ran the many special effects visitors enjoyed during their day at the park.

The vintage flavor of the street reminded her of the thirties and forties. Of course, Carlie loved it; it made her think of the many old films she liked so much.

But that had been in daylight. In the dark, the street struck her as sinister, dangerous. Like this, it reminded her of the old-time gangsters, the mob in its flamboyant heyday. And Carlie no longer found it amusing. It had all become too real when she'd uncovered the truth behind the privileged life she'd lived.

Another shiver shook her.

These days, she much preferred reality to illusions that were more smoke and mirrors than anything else.

Dan tugged at her hand. "What? Did you freeze on me?"

She shook her head—and shook the ruminations from her mind. "No. Just watching a bunch of strange thoughts cross my mind."

"Let's go. I want to check out the *Revenge of the Mummy* attraction. I don't remember what the structure is like inside. Maybe we can bunk down there."

"How about *Men in Black?*"

"*Back to the Future?*"

"No! I got it. Let's go to *Shrek*. It's a theater, and the seats were decent."

"Good idea. I think we might get some sleep there."

When they'd reentered the gates they'd gone straight down the main street to the New York area, and so now they had to make a U-turn and head back up a street parallel to the one they'd just come down.

Clang! Rattle! Bump!

Carlie's pulse shot higher than before. She couldn't draw a breath. They'd been found.

She dug her nails into Dan's hand.

His hand convulsed around hers. "Don't move," he whispered.

Then she spotted the source of the racket. Partway to *Shrek,* three maintenance workers came out of a store. The noise of their cleaning paraphernalia tore the quiet of the night. Dan and Carlie pressed up tighter against the wall of the nearest building, hoping the shadows there would keep their presence secret.

The two women and one man trundled off oblivious to Dan and Carlie, their chitchat melodious in the way of native Spanish speakers. Then Carlie looked at the building the workers had just cleaned.

"Looks like things might be going our way," she said. "They just left *Shrek.*"

"I'll wait until we can get inside before I agree with your Pollyanna assessment."

"Hey! Aren't you trained in picking locks and all that kind of thing?"

"That only happens in movies, Carlie. This is real life. I can't just barge into private property. That's not what I'm trained to do."

"No, but something tells me you know how to pick a lock."

He looked away, and then shook his head. "Yeah, I know how to pick a lock. And if worse comes to worst, I'll do it."

Carlie stifled a yawn. "I think worse has come to worst. I'm about to fall asleep on my feet. Let's go find us a pair of theater seats."

Of course, he had to pick the lock. But once he did, they were in and down the aisles in minutes. "Pick a seat," he said, waving, "any seat. Your wish is my command."

Carlie gave him a sad smile. "My wish is for an end to this weird life I've been living." Then she called on the Lord to strengthen her inner reserves, and took a deep breath. "Since you can't do a thing to change that, I'll just take…hmm…that seat over there."

Carlie's pick was an aisle seat. Dan picked its adjacent companion. They sat, wriggled in an attempt to get comfortable. Both soon gave up on that. Instead, they sought relief for their feet. Dan propped his long legs on the back of the seat in front of his. Carlie followed suit.

"Night," she mumbled.

"Good night, Carlie."

Seconds later, Carlie's eyelids grew heavy and her head drooped. She'd never know if she dreamt it or if it really happened, but she felt Dan's arm wrap around her shoulders, and his large, warm hand cup her cheek.

"Mmm…" she murmured.

He responded by pressing her head onto his

shoulder. Carlie had the impression of strength, tenderness, and yes, even love.

Against all odds, she felt better, maybe even safer, in that awkward theater seat than she ever had since the day the bullets hit Carlo and changed her life forever.

She had no doubt it was because of Dan's comforting presence at her side, this man she'd begun to suspect the Lord had allowed in her path for a reason.

"Thank You, Father," she whispered and curled in closer to Dan's warmth.

SEVENTEEN

When Dan's watch alarm rang at 5:00 a.m., he found his arms wrapped around Carlie. In turn, she'd wrapped one of hers around his chest, while her head still rested on his shoulder. The depth of emotion that filled him took his breath away. He could get used to waking up next to her.

Did he want to? Did he care that much for her?

Was he in love?

Did he see marriage in their future?

His heart skipped a beat, and in the silence of the morning, he turned to his fledgling prayer abilities.

Lord? Did You bring us together? As unlikely as we seem, I think she stole my heart. I'm not sure what to do...what is right. Carlie, J.Z. and David all say You'll show me the way, that You'll guide me. I'm ready. Show me what to do.

As sweet a feeling as he had right then, he knew he couldn't relish it much longer; he couldn't let more time go by. Park attendants would arrive soon to prepare for the day ahead, and he and Carlie had to leave the theater before someone came inside. Where they would go, he didn't know yet, but he prided himself on his ability to think on his feet.

Carlie's life depended on it these days.

A greater sense of urgency overtook him. Why? He didn't know. Was it because he'd accepted his feelings for Carlie? Was it because David's and J.Z.'s presence in Orlando emphasized the danger? Or was it because, having now turned to God in faith, he felt a responsibility to someone greater than himself? The FBI?

In any case, he didn't have the luxury to sit there and ponder all his questions. He had to get them out of harm's way—again.

"Carlie…" He ran a gentle finger down her cheek. "Please wake up. We have to get out of here before someone finds us."

Her long eyelashes fluttered, and then her eyes opened. Dan watched, looked into the chocolate depths. He smiled at the disorientation she revealed.

"Morning, sleepyhead."

"It's not morning yet. It's still dark."

"It's morning, all right, early morning. But it's dark because we're still inside the *Shrek* theater. Come on. We have to get out of here."

He could almost see the details clicking into place in Carlie's mind. Once they did, she glanced down, realized how closely they were entangled, and withdrew from his embrace. He noticed the blush on her cheeks.

"Uh…let's go," she said. "I'm ready to face whatever today throws at us."

As she stepped into the aisle, Dan caught her hand. "When I'm sure you're safe, we're going to have to have a talk. A serious talk, and it won't have anything to do with your family, moles, or even theme parks."

Her eyes grew wide, she shivered, and her mouth formed a perfect *O,* but she didn't say a word. Instead, she pulled her hand from his, and started up the aisle. At the door, she paused.

"What next? Where will we go?"

"I'll have to figure this out on the fly. I don't know much about how this place runs, so we'll have to keep an eye out for workers. I'm not sure how we'll be able to dodge them, but that's going to be the key until the gates open."

"What about J.Z. and David? Will they be coming out here again? How will we know they're here?"

He shot her a grin. "Full of questions, aren't you?" When she shrugged, he continued. "They're going to follow up on the mole. They were planning to see Sonia and look into any information she's gathered. Then they'll come find us."

"How will we know they're here? Did J.Z. leave us his walkie-talkie?"

"They rented a locker for me last night before they left. Apparently, it's not strange for people to do that when they plan to return the next day. I have one of the keys, and we left the radio there. I'll pick it up, together with any information David or J.Z. might leave for us, once the crowds fill this place again. They'll meet us in the early evening."

"That makes me feel a little better. The thought of

being stuck here, all alone, with who knows who after us, is not especially comforting, you know?"

Again, Dan caught Carlie's hand. "What happened to that strong faith of yours? I'm trying to believe, and now I'm going to encourage you not to stop. Let's trust God, let's believe He'll pull us through."

For a moment, she kept silent. Then she nodded and squeezed his hand. "You're right. I have to trust the Lord."

They retraced their steps of the night before down a street they'd enjoyed until they spotted the shadow by the car. Now, however, they reacted differently. Every so often, Dan stole peeks at Carlie. It didn't take him long to figure out that her exuberant joy of the day before was gone.

She now looked apprehensive; she darted glances in all directions; her posture looked strained, tight, as though she were ready for flight. Which Dan hoped she was, since he feared it would come to that at one point or another.

He hoped it would be after his colleagues returned.

Time seemed to slow down to a crawl when groups of park attendants appeared. Carlie and Dan scrambled for places to hide. Shrubs, trash bins, the backs of buildings, all served a purpose.

Finally, when they'd exhausted their choices for hiding, nine o'clock arrived. The usual hordes of tourists poured in, and Carlie and Dan breathed easier. But Carlie didn't display the same effervescence she had.

"Thank me, Carlie," he said to tease her into a better mood. "You get an extra day at the park."

She slanted him a look. "Sorry, but it's not the same.

And I'm worried about the others. They've come to Orlando to help me, but now they're in danger, too. And I miss Frisbee."

They fell silent again, and Dan chose a couple of attractions to visit. But while the day before, Carlie had seemed insatiable when it came to exploring the park, now Dan had to tug her along in his wake.

"Come on," he urged later on. "We're going to draw attention if we just sit here and stare at the front gate. We have the walkie-talkie—" he waggled the gadget "—and they'll let us know as soon as they arrive."

She let him drag her from attraction to attraction, and he felt his heart break at the sadness on her face. Something she'd enjoyed the day before, had now become drudgery, frightening, dangerous. Not for the first time, Dan felt his anger grow.

The hours dragged along in the same, frustrating way.

His anger continued to increase. He didn't know if it was directed at her father, her brother, or her late husband, or if instead, he was mad at himself and the Philly office. They'd done a poor job of protecting her. She was supposed to be in a safe-house, but the safe-house had become a death trap. Looking back on all that had happened, it was a good thing she'd insisted on park-hopping. Otherwise, he feared she already would be dead.

Or would she?

They still hadn't uncovered the identity of the mole, nor did they fully understand his motives. Maybe the mole had a reason for keeping her alive, as they'd thought before. Was it all about the money? Maybe the attacks had only meant to frighten Carlie, to keep her off-kilter, to prepare her for…for what? For divulging the location of the missing millions when finally confronted?

Dan let out a frustrated sound, unintelligible and unsatisfying, but one he'd been powerless to stifle.

And then, just as the stress became practically unbearable, the walkie-talkie crackled to life. "Yeah," he said into the mike.

"We saw Sonia," J.Z. said. "Meet us at Richter's Burger Company. It's in the San Francisco/Amity area of the park. You know, way at the back. We need to talk. Snag a table, okay?"

Dan and Carlie hurried. They arrived out of breath, and huffed and puffed to a table. After a quick look at the menu, they each ordered cheeseburgers and sodas, hoping J.Z. and David would arrive soon.

The men reached their table as Dan took a bite of his burger. He gestured toward the empty chairs, chewed then swallowed. "These are great. Join us."

David and J.Z. swapped looks. Dan didn't like their expressions. He gulped down a mouthful of soda. "Okay. I've known you both for a pretty long time. Something's up. Spill it."

J.Z. picked up a spoon and used it to draw on a napkin. "Whoever's turned is good. And probably holds a fairly high-up position."

"And…?"

"What do you mean, and? Isn't that bad enough?"

"I figured that out a while ago. He has access to just about everything. Maybe Eliza's assistant? Think Larry would sell out? She'll have his head on a platter if he did.

Or do you think it's someone above her? Above Tom Marcum? She thinks the world of him as a boss, and she's a tough stickler, so I don't think it'd be him."

"We have our suspicions," David answered. "And Sonia's checking on a couple more things."

Carlie plunked down her condensation-damp soda cup. "So basically, we're no further along than we were yesterday."

"Further along on what?" a woman asked.

J.Z. groaned.

David shook his head.

Dan rubbed his forehead, blinked, but still saw their boss at tableside. "What are you doing here, Eliza?"

"Can't a woman take a vacation?" the redhead asked.

"Right where I've taken a witness? Where we've been followed, in spite of my efforts otherwise? Right where we suspect a mole has again revealed our location?"

Eliza arched a brow. "Mole? You guys are on that kick again? Can't you get it through your heads that I run a tight ship? No one, you hear? No one in my office turns. I don't tolerate it."

J.Z. squinted at Eliza. "And you believe you can control everyone? Hate to break the news, Eliza, but you're not that powerful."

She scowled. "Don't bet on it, J.Z."

"I don't bet, I trust in God. And I know only He has that kind of power. Like the song says, He does hold the whole world in His hands."

"Pfft!" She gave a dismissive wave. "Marriage doesn't become you. You've become too provincial since you hooked up with your little librarian. And if anything, even more insubordinate. Don't forget. I can fire you anytime."

Even though Dan knew how much J.Z. loved his career, he watched his partner shrug. "I'm not worried. I have another boss Who'll see me through."

Dan didn't need any more sparring. "So what's the point of your visit, Eliza? Do you have information for us?"

She shrugged. "Not really. I'm on vacation, as I already said."

"Then if you don't mind," he went on, "we'd like to get back to our lunch, and you should return to your vacation."

"Oh…that's right," she said in a falsely offhand way. "I do have a bit of business. You're off the case, Dan. You were only supposed to escort Ms. Papparelli to Orlando. The Federal Marshals are supposed to have custody of her now. What did you do with the woman assigned to the job?"

"I did nothing. She's investigating the mole you're so sure doesn't exist."

Eliza placed a red-nailed finger on her cheek. "Let's see. The Marshal's supposed to protect the witness. You're an investigating Special Agent, but you're still hovering over Ms. Papparelli. Doesn't that strike you as backwards?"

"Sonia and I agreed this would work better."

"But *I* wasn't consulted, and I don't think it does. Get back to the office, Maddox. Immediately."

"Or else…?"

"You know. Or else you can kiss your job goodbye. So what'll it be?"

"I'll think about it, and call you in the morning."

She drew a sharp breath. "Then I guess the call won't be necessary. You're fired."

As angry as he was, Dan still felt as though she'd landed a fist in his gut. But he didn't let his response show. "Then I'm going to enjoy an Orlando vacation—with my friends."

J.Z. stood and faced Eliza. "Don't you think you'd better leave?"

Eliza glared back. "I think I can decide what I do. Or would you like to join your partner in the ranks of the unemployed? Insubordination, you understand."

J.Z. didn't answer right away. The moments dragged by. Then he met Dan's gaze before he turned back to their boss. "You know, Eliza? I think this might be the right moment after all. I think I'm with Dan. An Orlando vacation followed by a job search sounds pretty good to me."

Her lips tightened, and Dan wondered if she was about to stomp her foot in a tantrum. But she didn't. She turned to David instead. "How about you? Are you in on their group resignations?"

David chuckled. "Now that I think about it, it sounds pretty good to me."

J.Z. crossed his arms. "I don't think you're really ready for this, Eliza. You tried to throw your weight around, but you didn't count on our lack of fear. Now you're at a loss. I'd suggest you get back to whatever you were doing before you tracked us down. Maybe a meeting in the office in a week or two would make more sense."

She narrowed her blue eyes. "Whatever else you three do, make sure Sonia Mendez is back on the job immediately. And she'd better stay in touch." She pointed to Carlie. "This woman's due to testify sometime in the future, and Mendez had better keep her alive and kicking. I'm not sure the Marshal is as ready to give up gainful employment as the rest of you are."

J.Z. grinned unexpectedly. "You know? Probable unemployment feels pretty good. Bye, Eliza. See ya in a couple of weeks."

She spun on the heel of her wedge-shaped sandals, and stormed off. Only then did Dan glance at Carlie. She looked stunned. Her jaw gaped. Her eyes had opened so wide that they looked as big as golf balls.

"Are you okay?" he asked.

"Me?" she squeaked. "I'm fine, but you guys are nuts! You just lost your jobs. All because of me."

"Nope," J.Z. countered. "All because of Eliza's nasty nature. She's had this…this *thing* against me ever since I decided I couldn't date a woman like her any longer. Unfortunately, these guys got caught up in her fits of temper. Still, I'm not sure she really meant what she said."

"But what will you do if she did?"

David shrugged. "We'll figure something out. Maybe we'll go into business together."

Dan's head spun with the events of the last few minutes. He let out a whistle. "Whoa! We have to keep one thing in mind. Carlie's still in danger. And we don't know where the next attack's going to come from."

Carlie leaned forward. "When are you guys going to check in with Sonia? Maybe she's figured out something."

"We'll check with her," Dan said. "But first we need to decide where to stash you. It's obvious you can't stay at the park indefinitely."

"Maybe Sonia can help." Carlie hoped so. "She knows the area pretty well."

As the evening deepened, they discussed possible hiding places, possible new careers, Eliza's unappealing personality and the dents Maryanne and Lauren might have made on bank accounts during their shopping spree that afternoon.

They were waiting for the cover of dark to leave the park. They hoped to draw less attention that way. They weren't the typical tourist group; three men and one woman didn't fit in with the more typical mom-dad-and-three-kid pods that migrated in streams along the streets.

During a lull in their conversation, Carlie cleared her throat. "Um…what are we going to do about Frisbee?"

The men groaned.

"I'd forgotten about the mutt," Dan groused. "I don't think he's the best idea. Why don't we take him to an animal shelter so they can find him a new home?"

Her sudden tears caught him off guard. "No!" she cried. "He's all I have left. He's my family now, and I won't give him away."

Somewhere deep in his heart, Dan felt a silent cry bubble up. *What about me? Can I be your family, too?*

His unexpected need was so great, that Dan's determination strengthened even more. "I'm sorry. You're right. Frisbee comes with us. We'll figure it out as we go along."

"We?" she asked through the veil of tears.

"What?" he asked, forcing a teasing tone into his words. "Did you think you'd get rid of me that easy?"

She looked down at her hands then back up and met his gaze. "Actually, I *was* afraid you'd disappear. It seems I've…" She grinned then hummed.

"I know that one!" He joined her hums, then broke into song. "'I've grown accustomed to her face….'"

J.Z. and David traded looks. Then David gave Dan a dopey look. "If you're singing show tunes, then you're in real trouble, my man."

Dan met his gaze. "I know. But it's okay."

J.Z. laughed. "He's in trouble, all right. And so are we—of a different kind. We'd better get them somewhere safe. And we should check on the progress of the trial. At least a tentative date should've been set by now…."

They left the restaurant and headed for the front gates. The sun had just slipped down past the edge of the horizon, and the sky had turned a clear, midnight blue. The temperature had dropped to a more comfortable range, and the tropical breeze felt great after the heat of the day.

They approached the lake that ran down the approximate middle of the park, and noticed a crowd gathering along the fence.

"They must be starting the powerboat stunt show," Carlie murmured.

Dan caught a hint of longing in her voice. "Do you want to watch some of it?"

Her expression lightened. "Could we?"

J.Z. shook his head.

David said "Hmm…"

Dan said, "Sure. We won't stay long, and then we can head on out."

Carlie placed a hand on his forearm. "Thanks."

They had to walk a ways along the fence to find an empty spot from which to watch the show. They wound up close to the powerboat launch dock. Dan stood behind Carlie, careful to cover her with his body. If anyone had tracked them down, just as Eliza had done, he wanted to make sure to protect her.

Moments later, the first of the boats roared to life. It sped across the surface, and threw out a five-foot arc of silver water in its wake. The spray sparkled and reflected the light from the floods ranged around the lake. Another boat shot across from the opposite side.

Overhead, fireworks burst into multicolored flowers, stars, horsetail sprays of red, blue, white, gold lights. The crowd cheered. The vessels crossed paths. One veered, turned back, sped after the other.

Shots rang out.

More fireworks blasted light against the night sky.

Dan, J.Z., and David reacted automatically. Each went for his gun. Carlie laughed. "Calm down, guys. It's just a show."

Dan gave a nervous laugh, but didn't let his weapon go. He noticed the others did the same.

And then, with a hideous hiss, a bullet sped past the right side of his head. *"Down!"* he roared. "Everybody down."

J.Z. turned to the family at his left. Dan heard him urge them to take cover.

Another spray of shots burst by.

David yelled, "FBI! Everyone get down."

Shots burst from what seemed like every direction.

That's when Dan noticed the stain on his fingers. It oozed out from Carlie's shoulder.

She collapsed in his arms.

EIGHTEEN

Something stung Carlie's shoulder, and the oomph of whatever it was pushed her back into Dan. They went down together. The stung spot hurt. "Ouch—"

"Carlie…!"

The anguish in his wail stunned her. She glanced over her shoulder, and read desperation in his face. "Dan! What's wrong? Are you hurt, too?"

His pale features eased fractionally. "You're alive!"

"Of course I'm alive. What's wrong with you?"

"What do you mean, what's wrong with me? You were just shot. There's blood all over you…all over me, now."

She gave her shoulder a tentative twitch. "Now that you mention it, my shoulder does hurt a lot. But it can't be too bad. I can still talk."

Overhead, another barrage of bullets split the night.

"Stay down." He eased her off his lap. "I've got to get him…whoever he is."

"What if they hurt you, too?"

"So be it, but I have to get this guy. I have to make

sure you're safe. One way or another, this can't go on any longer."

"Dan—"

Carlie cut off her words. He'd left. Fear threatened, so instead of giving in, she turned to prayer.

"Father, go with him. He's so dedicated, but bullets don't know about good-hearted, dedicated men. Protect him, and if it's Your will, give us a chance to have that conversation he talked about."

She looked around, then gasped. She was alone. Where had all the other tourists gone? Where were Dan, J.Z. and David? Had the gunmen also gone?

Carlie's heart pounded in her chest. From the left and over the lake, another spurt of gunfire exploded. Okay. So they weren't gone. She felt pretty certain the real show had come to an abrupt end.

As the moments crept by, the pain in her shoulder increased. She had to do something about the wound. Bullets and the holes they made weren't the healthiest things to mess around with.

But Carlie didn't want to stand and draw attention to herself. She wasn't stupid. With smooth, cautious movements, Carlie began to make her way along the fence toward the front of the park. If there was one thing she knew, it was that she couldn't stay where she'd fallen. Sooner or later, whoever had shot her would come to make sure they'd met their goal.

"Psst!"

Carlie jerked and scrabbled forward.

"It's me," Dan hissed. "Come on."

"You've got to stop scaring me like that!"

"This isn't the time to argue. Just follow. David and J.Z. went toward the front of the park. They're drawing attention away from us."

"How do you plan to get us out of here?"

"They're calling backup, but you and I are going by water."

"You want me to swim with a bullet hole in my shoulder?"

"No. We're taking one of the speedboats."

The idea had a certain appeal. Then something occurred to her. "Do you know how to run one of those things?"

"I know how to drive a car."

"Oh, that inspires a world of confidence—"

"Stop! I know you chatter when you're nervous or scared, but this isn't the time. We have to get out of here before they come after us again."

This time, the urgency in his voice got through to Carlie. She shoved her fears aside, pushed the pain to a far corner of her mind, and called on the Lord for courage and cover from those who'd come after them—her.

They retraced the short span of fence Carlie had skirted before Dan returned. At the end of the shrubs and wire, she finally saw the dock. A sleek, cigarette-type race boat sat there, almost as if waiting for them. No attendants were anywhere to be seen.

Carlie and Dan scrambled into the powerboat. He went straight to the steering wheel, while she collapsed on a seat. It wasn't the most comfortable chair in the house, so to speak, but her shoulder had begun to throb.

"Where are we going?" she asked. "If I remember correctly, this lake is more of a large pond. It doesn't really go anywhere."

"All I want to do is get you past the shooter and closer to the park exit. There's a first aid station near the gate. You need help."

"She needs more than help," Eliza said, a gun in her hand. She too boarded the boat. "Ms. Papparelli needs to cough up the cash."

Carlie gaped.

Dan frowned.

Eliza stepped toward Dan. The boat rocked. Carlie shuddered.

"Start the engine," Eliza commanded.

Carlie watched Dan control his anger, although in the moonlight, she also caught the tensing of a muscle in his cheek.

"And then what?" he asked his former boss, his voice cool and even.

"Don't worry about that. I'll take care of what comes next."

Carlie gulped. She had a pretty good idea what Eliza had in mind for next.

"But…why?" she asked.

Eliza turned on her. "Four million dollars—excuse me, *five* million dollars—speak for themselves."

Dan turned the key someone, more than likely the attendant who should have driven this third boat in the show, had left in the ignition. The motor rumbled right up.

"You sold out the Bureau for money?" Dan asked.

Eliza laughed. "Don't sound so shocked. There's more to life than catching so-called 'bad guys,' Dan."

"The *finer* things, I suppose."

"Something like that."

"And people don't matter."

She shrugged. "You're asking too many questions. And since I watch enough bad TV, I know you're trying to buy time. I'm not about to spill any beans, and even if I did, it wouldn't matter. Your future's certain."

Carlie stifled a groan. That didn't sound good. She did, however, have one question, one she thought she could get Eliza to answer. "Are you helping my father? Tony? Or maybe Larry Gemmelli? Which one got to you?"

"None of them, really. They just inspired me." Eliza gave a harsh laugh. "Here's a song I'm sure you, with your passion for old movies, will remember. I just sing it my way. 'Anything they can do, I can do better. I can do anything better than they…'"

Dan shot her a look. "You've become a mob of one."

"Not exactly. I just stepped into a void."

"A void?" Dan asked. "What kind of void did you find? The only void I know is the one left by Papparelli's death and the arrests of the Verdis, Larry Gemmelli, and Ric DiStefano and his pagan pals. Are you saying you've taken over the reins of their portion of the Philadelphia mob?"

"I told you I wasn't talking, and I'm not. Speed it up. This is a race boat, after all. And the lake's not big. Puttering on the water's not an option."

"You're in a hurry, then."

"I have plans for you two. I'm anxious to carry them out."

Carlie met Dan's gaze. In the glow of a nearby flood-light, she saw his lips move. "Pray…"

She did just that.

Dan's anger knew no bounds. Eliza had fooled them well. With her stiff-necked attitude and straight-arrow management style, no one had considered her a candidate for possible traitor—to his regret. And Carlie might pay for his blindness.

Although he'd always relied on his own abilities, those abilities had now hit a brick wall. He couldn't even count on David and J.Z.; they were busy following the shooters on the other boats, and calling up help. And while he hadn't had much time to study a Bible since he'd taken a chance on God, he did know a few of its most famous stories—at least one.

He now knew how Daniel had felt in the lions' den.

As if it hadn't been bad enough to begin with, their situation had taken a turn for the desperate, courtesy of the mob, Eliza, and her greed. Funny how an open-top powerboat could feel so much like a den. Unfortunately, Carlie was stuck here, too, injured and dependent on him.

How would he ever get them out of this bad B-movie-like mess? How would he manage to keep Carlie alive? He had no illusions about Eliza's compassion—she had none.

He couldn't stand to think of losing Carlie. Not now that he'd accepted his feelings for her, not now that he knew he wanted what J.Z. and David had found with the women they loved.

But how? How was he going to get them out of this?

Then he knew. He wasn't. He couldn't. Not on his own.

It was in that boat, with a gun pointed at his head, that Dan finally understood what his new brothers in faith and Carlie had tried to tell him time and time again. He wasn't an island alone. God had sent him help in the form of his colleagues, and he'd almost turned it down.

"Move, Dan," Eliza ordered.

As tough as she liked to appear, he still caught a note of anxiety in her voice. Maybe she wasn't as in command of her situation as she wanted him and Carlie to believe. There had to have been more than one gunman. Had she commandeered a boat? Or had her accomplices handled that? Was she afraid of those accomplices? If so, he might be able to use her fear to his advantage.

Playing dumb seemed like the thing to do. "I'm doing my best."

And he was. He was doing his best to hang on to his fragile, new faith—he had no other choice—and to think things through to a logical, safe end. In a moment of revelation, he recognized his inadequacy.

Lord? he prayed silently. *I finally understand. I can't do anything on my own to save myself—to save us. Please help! Don't let Carlie pay for my pride. I'll trust You. We can count on my training. Please do Your part...whatever that might be. Oh! And Amen.*

Another burst of gunfire whizzed over their boat, and Dan had one of his answers. Eliza blanched. Her pals weren't done.

Carlie moaned.

"Were you hit again?" he asked, his heart pounding with fear.

"No! They just came too close—"

"Shut up!" Eliza cried. "Now! Get me to the dock."

Carlie's eyes looked like bottomless pools in pale sand. Her fear was so great, that Dan felt he could almost touch it. Then she closed her eyes, lowered her head, and prayed again.

He faced forward, spotted the other dock not more than fifty feet ahead. Out the corner of his eye, he caught Eliza's movement toward the side of the boat. She was anxious to disembark. He again had to wonder how confident she felt when dealing with mob lowlifes.

Before he knew what had happened, Carlie erupted from where she'd sat, lunged for Eliza, planted her hands on the other woman's back, and gave her a shove. Eliza screamed, the gun flew from her hand, and she went overboard. The gun splashed down, too.

Dan grinned. "Way to go!"

"Hit it, Dan!"

He did. In seconds, they reached the dock. To his relief, the only people there were David, J.Z. and an EMT. Although she gave him a hard time about "dumping" her, Dan handed Carlie over to the medic, pressed a kiss on her forehead, and promised to be right back for her once the rest of Eliza's cronies were rounded up.

He and his colleagues divided the labor. J.Z., Eliza's once-upon-a-time flame, would wait for the water-logged traitor, then hand her over to the authorities, who, thankfully, were on their way. Dan and David still had her accomplices to track down.

"But you can't just leave me behind!" Carlie wailed. "I can help! I'm the one who knocked Eliza off the boat, aren't I? Let me come along…"

As he took off to find Eliza's buddies, Dan tossed a glance over his shoulder. He chuckled. Carlie was in fine form. The EMT struggled to tend to her wound, while the love of his life batted at the poor woman's hands.

"Carlie Papparelli!" he yelled. "You crazy woman! I love you. Will you marry me?"

That was all it took. Her mouth gaped; her eyes opened wide; her hands dropped to her sides. The medic went to work.

"And just so you know?" he added. "I'm not joking. I mean every word I just said."

As he pelted after David, he heard her call out, "I love you, too, and I'll kill you if you get yourself killed."

He laughed. And thanked God.

The Lord really did work in mysterious ways.

Three weeks later all six were back in Philly. Carlie had to testify against Eliza before a grand jury, and David and Lauren had a wedding to plan.

Dan and Carlie also had a conversation that had been put on hold long enough. But no matter how often she tried to lead Dan in that direction, it seemed he wouldn't be led. Had he forgotten his proposal? Had it only been a means to an end? Had he really wanted to shut her up that much?

Or did he have a plan?

Carlie had just finished her third day before the grand jury, and was waiting for Dan to come pick her up. He'd suggested they go to dinner, and Carlie's hopes had taken flight. Maybe…

He showed up in his latest bland beige Bureau car.

"Don't you own a vehicle of your own?" she asked as she clicked on her seat belt.

His blue eyes twinkled. "I have a Harley. Would you rather ride that to the restaurant?"

She gaped. "A Harley? One of those huge, noisy, scary monster bikes?"

Dan laughed. "It's not that scary. I'm a good driver. Never had even one bobble in all the years I've had it."

"How many years have you had it?"

"Since I graduated high school.'

"That's a long time."

"I tend to hang on to the things I like."

Something in the tone of his voice told Carlie that he'd meant more than what the simple words seemed to say. A thrill of excitement ran through her. She sent a quick prayer for courage heavenward.

"Anything else you've hung on to for a while?" she asked, emboldened.

He turned the corner, pulled into a vacant spot by a parking meter, and turned off the car. In a slow, deliberate way, he twisted in his seat and faced her. His smile sent a shiver right through her.

"Yeah," he drawled. "There's something I've kept around for…oh, a long time."

Carlie's heart picked up its beat. "And it's something you like?"

"Oh, I do. Like it, that is. A lot."

"And you plan to keep it around for a while longer?"

"Try the rest of my life."

"Hmm…sounds intriguing."

"I hope so." He slipped his left hand in his pocket then, with his right, reached out for her left. "What do you say?"

Carlie stared at the beautiful ruby-and-diamond ring. "It's different."

"So are you." He slipped the piece onto her ring finger. "So, does it work?"

She turned her hand around and wove her fingers through his. "Only if it comes with a promise attached."

"I promise to cherish you, protect you and love you for the rest of my life. How about you?"

Through the knot in her throat and the tears in her eyes, Carlie said, "I promise to honor you, support you and love you for the rest of my life."

He leaned forward and kissed her lips. Carlie's tears fell, dampened his cheeks.

"I hope those are tears of joy," he murmured.

"Of course."

"So you'll marry me?"

"When?"

"Valentine's Day?"

"Works for me."

"I love you, Carlie."

"I love you, too."

They sealed their promise with another kiss.

In the following months, Carlie and Dan attended David and Lauren's wedding, and prepared for their own. They began to pray together; they worked together to turn a house they bought into their future home; they played with Frisbee, and they came to treasure the peace they found as they trusted God.

Soon enough, February arrived. The fourteenth found Dan at the altar, waiting for his bride. David and J.Z. took their places at his side. Beautiful music filled the sanctuary. Then the procession began. He took two steps forward, anticipating Carlie's appearance.

First came six-year old Mark DiStefano, in his hands a satin pillow holding two rings. A pregnant Maryanne Prophet followed, and stood at J.Z.'s side. The last attendant, a radiant Lauren Latham, glided up the aisle and went straight to her brand-new spouse.

Finally, *finally,* Dan's bride approached. "Thank You, Father," he breathed. "For bringing her into my life, for protecting her, and for the peace she showed me I would find in You."

Minutes later Dan pledged himself as God's servant and Carlie's partner for as long as they both would live.

* * * * *

Dear Reader,

My memories of visits to theme parks as a child begin with our arrival the moment the gates opened. Then we'd hit every attraction in the park, and finally we'd leave when the employees were ready to dropkick us to our car in the vast, by-then-empty parking lot. My dad enjoyed every second of the day, and made sure we did, too!

I married a man with the same approach to theme-park vacations, and our sons have grown up with the same memories. For that reason, theme parks mean family vacations to me, and it was during one a few years ago that the idea for *Married to the Mob* occurred to me. I count my blessings daily, and am especially grateful for the extended "family" my career has brought me. I hope you enjoy Carlie's visits to the parks, and that my work blesses you, as your letters do me.

In Him,

Ginny Aiken

QUESTIONS FOR DISCUSSION

1. Carlie had to start over again, both as a new Christian and as a woman in the witness protection program. What kind of spiritual challenge would that present you?

2. When faced with the realization that many of his colleagues believe he has betrayed the FBI, Dan turns to God. If you were in a similar situation, how would you respond?

3. Believing she has little time to live, Carlie wants to visit the Orlando theme parks before she dies. Are there things you would want to accomplish if you also had very little time left on earth? What would they be?

4. Dan is understandably proud of his accomplishments as an FBI agent. Do you have accomplishments that bring you a similar sense of success and satisfaction? What are they?

5. If you had to relocate, where would you like to live? Why?

6. Are there aspects of your daily life that you would miss if you had to undergo a change like Carlie's? If so, what are they? If not, why not?

7. Carlie struggles with the restrictions Dan imposes on her daily life. How would you feel if you were in Carlie's place?

8. If you had to start a completely new life, what would you feel you had to bring along? Why?

A SEASON FOR GRACE

BY
LINDA GOODNIGHT

THE BROTHERS' BOND

**Separated as children...
reunited as men.**

Police officer and former
foster child Collin Grace
wasn't fond of social
workers, even pretty ones
like Mia Carano. But Mia
knew he was the perfect
mentor for a runaway in
her care—and she wouldn't
stop until she unearthed
the caring man under
Collin's gruff exterior.

Steeple
Hill®

www.SteepleHill.com

*Available December 2006,
wherever you buy books.*

LOVE WALKED IN

BY

MERRILLEE WHREN

Getting close to new neighbor Clay Reynolds was not a consideration for single mom Beth Carlson. She had no time for romance. Clay was good to her son—and to her—but she could never give her heart to a motorcycle-riding man again. Or could she?

Available December 2006, wherever you buy books.

Steeple Hill®

www.SteepleHill.com

LILWI

REQUEST YOUR FREE BOOKS!

2 FREE INSPIRATIONAL NOVELS
PLUS 2
FREE
MYSTERY GIFTS

YES! Please send me 2 FREE Love Inspired® novels and my 2 FREE mystery gifts. After receiving them, if I don't wish to receive any more books, I can return the shipping statement marked "cancel." If I don't cancel, I will receive 4 brand-new novels every month and be billed just $3.99 per book in the U.S., or $4.74 per book in Canada, plus 25¢ shipping and handling per book and applicable taxes, if any*. That's a savings of at least 20% off the cover price! I understand that accepting the 2 free books and gifts places me under no obligation to buy anything. I can always return a shipment and cancel at any time. Even if I never buy another book from Steeple Hill, the two free books and gifts are mine to keep forever.

113 IDN EF26   313 IDN EF27

Name	(PLEASE PRINT)	
Address		Apt.
City	State/Prov.	Zip/Postal Code

Signature (if under 18, a parent or guardian must sign)

Order online at www.LoveInspiredBooks.com

Or mail to Steeple Hill Reader Service™:

IN U.S.A.	IN CANADA
P.O. Box 1867	P.O. Box 609
Buffalo, NY	Fort Erie, Ontario
14240-1867	L2A 5X3

Not valid to current Love Inspired subscribers.

Want to try two free books from another series?
Call 1-800-873-8635 or visit www.morefreebooks.com

* Terms and prices subject to change without notice. NY residents add applicable sales tax. Canadian residents will be charged applicable provincial taxes and GST. This offer is limited to one order per household. All orders subject to approval. Credit or debit balances in a customer's account(s) may be offset by any other outstanding balance owed by or to the customer. Please allow 4 to 6 weeks for delivery.

LIREG06

Love Inspired
SUSPENSE
RIVETING INSPIRATIONAL ROMANCE

Out of the Depths
VALERIE HANSEN

With vandals trying to destroy Trudy Lynn Brown's campground, she turned to her best friend's brother, Cody Keringhoven, to protect her property. Recently injured Cody didn't realize keeping Trudy Lynn safe from the culprits determined to bring her down just might cost him his heart.

Available December 2006,
wherever you buy books.

Steeple
Hill®

LISOOTD

Love Inspired .
SUSPENSE

TITLES AVAILABLE NEXT MONTH

Don't miss these two stories in December

OUT OF THE DEPTHS by Valerie Hansen

Trudy Lynn Brown needed someone to help her get rid of the vandals threatening her campground. Cody Keringhoven fit the bill, yet how can the recently injured Cody find the strength to protect her with criminals determined to drive her away?

THE INN AT SHADOW LAKE by Janet Edgar

Special Agent Zachary Marshall had tracked a deadly terrorist ring to a secluded resort—right to a woman he'd once loved. He found himself falling for Julie Anderson all over again, but was she a cunning traitor...or an innocent victim of ruthless criminals?